The
Lady
and the
GIANT

The
Lady
and the
GIANT

* * * * * * *

Clarence Budington Kelland

* * * * * * *

Dodd, Mead & Company
NEW YORK

The

Lady

and the

GIANT

* * 1 * *

LOSSIE and I sat under the big elm between our twin houses on James Street. It seems not to have been uncommon in the days when our homes were erected, for brothers or close friends to build identical homes side by side, and this is what our fathers had done. They were close friends and partners, and if a stranger asked their business, they would reply that they were salt boilers. Which, indeed, they were, for the production of salt was, perhaps, the principal industry of Syracuse in the '60's.

Our homes were of red brick, square, and each was topped by a cupola. Fine doorways with fanlights stood behind Doric columns, and on each door was a silver plate bearing the name of the owner. On our door the name was Applegate, and on Lossie's door the name was Fox.

Across the street in a spacious yard stood a fine Corinthian-style house but newly tenanted after a year of vacancy, and by a mysterious and beautiful lady, arrived suddenly out of the nowhere to take residence after a flurry of renovation, painting and furnishing. Even the iron colored boy at the hitching block was shining in freshly painted red coat and white trousers and black boots.

This newest addition to our population created high curiosity and was the occasion of much whispering and speculation. That she was beautiful and stately could be observed by all; that she was wealthy was evidenced by her retinue and by the extremely handsome team of chestnut horses with coachman to drive them, which inhabited the stables. The coachman was liveried, as was the butler, at whom Lossie and I gazed with some awe.

Janeway was her name. It was accepted quickly that she was to be spoken of as Madam Cissie Janeway—though just how this came to be so was a mystery to us who were wholly unacquainted with that art which, many years later, came to be known as public relations. At any rate, even before we saw the lady, we had somehow been instructed that her name was Madam Cissie Janeway.

For some days after her arrival she was invisible, which was taken to be a sign of proper modesty and decorum. Then, each morning at ten, her open carriage drove around from the stables and Madam Janeway, dainty parasol in hand, tripped down the steps to the block and stepped into her equipage. She was of medium height, but seemed taller. She was possessed of a wonderful, lithe figure which she handled with consummate grace. Her little bonnet perched upon a coif of bronze hair. Her face was beautiful—almost Grecian—strikingly aristocratic and dignified. Her eyes were large and brown and very, very brilliant. Somehow one was impressed by the fact that her aristocracy was embellished by high intelligence. But also, there was something sweet and a little sad about her expression, and when she smiled one's heart went out to her. The envious guessed that she was in her later thirties; the unbiased opined that she might be in her closing twenties. The fact, not known until later days, was that she was forty-one.

Lossie had returned but the week before from her travels in Europe, and to my somewhat bewildered discomfort I found her not the tomboyish chum who had sailed away in June. Lossie was four years younger than I, being at that time in her nineteenth year. Whatever of hoyden there had been when she went away had been erased by contact with the culture of the Old World, and I was conscious of a restraint between us that never had been there before. Never, from that first day when I had been taken in to see her in her cradle, had we been anything but playmates; she the more daring and adventurous.

But this evening she was not a playmate; she was a lady. No longer was she a creature with scrawny legs and flying hair and smudged cheeks. She did not even look the same, and I, after studying the matter carefully, was dismayed to see that she was on the verge of becoming a beautiful woman. I wondered hopefully if this new, dignified, standoffish manner of hers was real or if it was something she had observed in foreign society and was practicing on me for mischief.

"There she is," Lossie said suddenly, and I looked

across the street to see Madam Janeway descend the front steps and walk across the front of the house to a garden where late flowers blossomed. She walked slowly, swaying a little as she walked, not looking about her and unaware that curious eyes might be studying her.

"She looks," I said, "like a queen."

Lossie sniffed. "She's giving us a chance to stare at her," she said.

"That," I said with that impoliteness which is used by children who are intimate, "is silly."

"She," snapped Lossie, "is making a parade."

"You're jealous," I said.

"You're a stupid boy. When you get to be a man you'll be more stupid."

"I am a man," I retorted. "I'm graduated from Cornell College and I'm admitted to the bar."

She looked at me and tittered, and I felt my cheeks flushing. Then she frowned. "Do you think she is beautiful?" Lossie asked, narrowing her eyes at me.

"Very handsome," I said shortly.

"Am I beautiful?" she demanded.

"Fiddlesticks," I told her. "You're just Lossie."

"Stupid!" she said with a shrug. And then, after a little pause while she scrutinized the lady across the street, "She's a hussy."

"Little girls," I said loftily, "mustn't be jealous. It makes them look silly."

"I don't feel like quarreling with you this evening," she said. "I suppose our mothers will be calling. They won't be able to restrain their curiosity. . . . Oh, oh,

4

there goes Banker Watts."

It was so. Banker Watts, wearing a tall beaver hat, was indeed turning up the walk toward Madam Janeway's door. She became aware of him and turned with a graceful gesture to greet him. She led the way up the steps and they disappeared inside the house.

Apparently Lossie dismissed our new neighbor from her thoughts. "Let's start early tomorrow morning," she said, with something of her old-time eagerness. "Did your father say you could have the horses?"

"Yes," I told her. "You're going to put up a lunch?"

We were going to the Onondaga Indian Reservation Fair, which we had attended every October since we were children. It was a great occasion, to be reached by going out the Cherry Valley Turnpike on the way to La Fayette village or to Cardiff if you turned to the right. Everybody went and wandered about all day among the booths, and bought Indian baskets and had a wonderful, tiresome time.

My mother called from our front porch, "Dinner's ready, Orrin," and I went in.

Only mother, father and I sat at table. Father asked the blessing and hardly had his amen been spoken when mother said in her brisk way, "Banker Watts just went in across the way—probably to supper."

"Probably business," father said.

"I thought," mother said, "that when people had business with bankers they went to the bank."

"Mrs. Janeway——" he commenced, but mother interrupted.

"Madam Janeway," she corrected.

Father grinned at her sardonically. "Madam Janeway is a new and important customer," he said. "Wealthy, I understand, and highly connected. It would be good business to pamper her some."

"Nellie and I are going to call," mother said. Nellie was Lossie's mother.

"I wouldn't rush things," father warned.

"Who," mother demanded, "are these important connections?"

"I had lunch with Watts today, and her name came up."

"I warrant it did," mother said ironically.

"He didn't mention names," father went on, "but you could tell he was impressed. Somebody pretty high up."

Mother sniffed in a way she had. "Probably the natural daughter of an earl," she said. "Why the mystery? If she's a member of some family like the Vanderbilts or the Goulds or Daniel Drews, why not come right out with it?"

"It was Watts who was reticent," father explained. "Acting like a banker!"

Mother changed the subject abruptly. It was a way she had. Her mind darted about, sometimes bewilderingly.

"You and Lossie are going to the Indian Fair?" she asked.

"Yes, mother."

"Foreign travel," mother said, "did Lossie good.

She's improved."

"It made her snippy," I complained.

"It'll wear off," father said carelessly. "I don't have to tell you to take good care of the horses."

"No, sir," I answered.

"When I was a boy," he told me, "my father didn't own a team worth a thousand dollars."

"Now, Silas!" mother warned, as she did every time father started in to tell us how he was a self-made man.

There was no formality about our supper. The roast was on a platter in front of father; the mashed potatoes were at his left. He sliced the meat and filled plates bountifully, dipping gravy on the potatoes and adding portions of mashed turnip. Mother served the peas in side dishes. We ate with appetite and without conversation. It was not until after the apple pie that father sighed and pushed back his chair. Mother arose and went into the kitchen; father went to his study, and I was at loose ends. As I passed father's study door I saw him tear the leaf from a large calendar over his desk and noted that tomorrow's date would be Saturday, October sixteenth, in the year 1869.

We breakfasted at six o'clock because father must be out at his salt-boiling plant at seven. Our barn man had the team hitched and ready, well before eight, and I called impatiently from the driver's seat to Lossie, who came out presently, followed by the cook carrying a basket of lunch. Lossie was irritated.

"You don't hoot and holler for a lady to come

out," she said tartly.

"Next time," I retorted, "I'll roll out a red carpet and hold a parasol over your head."

She scrambled between the wheels and settled herself beside me. "You are to stop treating me as if I were another boy," she said seriously. "I am a young lady."

"Fiddlesticks," I told her. "Even if you've been to Europe and come home with your nose in the air, you're still Lossie. So don't put on airs with me."

I clucked to the horses and swung them into the street. Lossie sulked for a little while, but as we reached the turnpike and I allowed the horses to trot briskly, her uppishness disappeared and her eyes glowed with eagerness and anticipation. She forgot that she was a fashionable young lady and became the Lossie of old.

It was not quite ten o'clock when we reached the entrance to the Indian Fair, but we could not turn in because the road was blocked by an excited crowd toward which people were running from all directions. In the middle of it stood a chubby man, muddy to the knees, who shouted and waved his hands and pranced.

I recognized him as one Gideon Emmons, who earned a living by doing odd jobs.

"I tell you all it's God's truth! Me and Henry Nicholls, we dug it up!" His voice broke to a sort of squeal. "It's a marvel of the world! It's a giant more'n forty feet long, all petrified and turned to stone! A great monster of a giant alayin' stretched in his grave. It's got arms 'n' laigs 'n' a face 'n' all like that! Me 'n' Henry we dug daown to it whilst we was diggin' a well fur Stubby Newell. Daown back of the barn on his Cardiff farm. It's a miracle, that's what it is, and nothin' like it's ever been seen in the world!"

"Is he drunk?" Lossie asked, gripping my arm.

"Don't look it," I said. "Could be some sort of a caper."

"So I come arunnin', leavin' Hank to guard it."

"If it's petrified," called a penetrating nasal voice, "it wouldn't run off. Not to speak of."

I recognized old David Hannum, banker and one of the slickest horse traders in the county.

"Let's go see," Lossie said eagerly, tugging at my sleeve.

The same idea struck the mob, and it streamed off down the road, more than a hundred of them at first, and then, as the news spread, scores of others as soon as they could hitch their rigs and get in motion. We turned down the road into the valley toward Cardiff, which was less than a hamlet. It really was the name of a place rather than a place. Two miles down this road we turned into the lovely, wooded valley, brilliant with crisp sunshine. Off to the west reared the green slope of Bear Mountain, and to eastward lifted the dark eminence of Pompey. Light clouds above threw their moving shadows down upon the mountain slope. And, somehow with suddenness, the great valley seemed somber and mysterious and portentous.

Lossie must have felt it because her fingers again gripped my arm and clung to it. It was a rough road, probably not passable at all after a rain, but we reached

Stubby Newell's farmhouse without mishap. We were among the first to arrive and to be confronted by bearded Henry Nicholls, important, but obviously awed.

"Keep back! Keep back 'n' be keerful!" he bellowed. "Don't cave her in!"

But the increasing crowd paid no attention. It trampled its way to a low spot behind the barn—a low, damp spot—and struggled for positions at the front.

"Land o' Goshen!" a subdued voice exclaimed. "Durned if it ain't!"

"Durned if it ain't what?" demanded a voice from the rear.

"A great, tarnation giant," said the first voice. "Bigger'n life 'n' twice as natural. All twisted, like he up 'n' died of a bellyache."

I managed to force a way through for Lossie. The crowd knew our fathers, so we were given some consideration. We stood at the crumbling brink of a pit some three feet deep, and there under our eyes was indeed a giant, not forty feet tall, as Gideon Emmons had said, but maybe a dozen feet in length. It lay upon its back and stared up at the sky out of sightless eyes. To me, in that moment, it seemed a noble, dignified face that I looked upon. Lossie clung to my arm and her lips were parted and her eyes wide.

"Pinch me, Orrin," she whispered. "This can't be so. I must be dreaming."

Careless of my Sunday-go-to-meeting suit of clothes, I leaped down into the excavation to examine the find more closely. It was almost entirely uncovered, but soft earth clung to it and required to be removed. I called for a broom, and in a moment one was passed down to me. I used it to clean the surface of the huge figure and disclosed the outer surface. Undoubtedly it was of stone, but I could detect no marks of a chisel. I bent closer and was able to see that which startled me mightily, for the entire body was covered, as the skin of a human being is covered, with pores. It was unthinkable. It was incredible. But this prima-facie evidence was an indication that this was no man-wrought statue, but the body of a petrified giant.

"What d'ye make it out to be, Orrin?" asked the nasal voice of David Hannum.

"I wouldn't want to say, sir," I answered. "But whatever it is, it's a marvel."

"Could it have been alive?" Lossie asked, as hands helped me to scramble out of the hole.

"If ever it was alive," I told her, "it died in agony. See how the body is distorted as though with pain."

The herd of humans pressing about the site of Newell's well was still—hushed with a sort of superstitious awe. It was a day, simple, primitive, when the casual possession of miracles such as were to come with the age of invention had not dulled the capacity of the human mind for astonishment. People, it seemed, preferred credulity to skepticism.

"Before we go messin' around," said a warning voice, "we better fetch a parson."

"Or"—Lossie's voice was suspiciously serious—

"the coroner."

"Lossie!" I rebuked.

"Isn't it the law?" she asked with innocent face. "If it's a man's body there'll have to be an inquest."

This was levity of which I could not approve. I frowned at her, but she was in no wise disconcerted. There had been times in the past—the more recent past —when Lossie had made me uncomfortable; times when I could not tell whether she was in earnest or joking. She would ask the most absurd questions with a straight face or make the most outrageous suggestions with childish naïveté. At times I was afraid she knew many things that it was not decorous for a girl to know, and at times she displayed a sort of innocent irreverence for serious matters that was upsetting. I know that I have a tendency to be overserious-minded, a matter of which she was inclined to take advantage.

By this time the Indian Fair must have been deserted, even by the Onondagas themselves. Everyone had scampered to witness this new marvel, and among the neck craners were a couple of parsons from neighboring towns. I did not know their names. Way was made for these authorities on the mysterious and unknown to approach the excavation, and there stood the two gentlemen of the cloth, staring down at the giant with expressionless faces. There came a little sound from Lossie which I was afraid was a titter.

"Which one'll win?" she whispered.

To me, it was apparent that neither preacher was eager to speak first; each waited cautiously for the other to take the risk of hazarding an opinion. The pause became painful, until at last one minister spoke ponderously, noncommittally.

"God," he said solemnly, "moves in a mysterious way His wonders to perform."

Lossie, distressingly irreverent, stood on tiptoe to reach my ear. "That," she said, "is what I call taking a firm and daring stand."

"Hush," I said uneasily, fearing she might be overheard.

The other minister clearly felt that he must not be outdone in this emergency by his brother. He was more specific, and uttered words which were to be quoted far and wide in the future by fundamentalists. "There were," he said pontifically, "giants in those days."

"Which days?" Lossie whispered.

"I think," said the first minister, after communion with himself, "that we should descend into the sepulcher and make closer examination."

So the two reverend gentlemen scrambled into the pit and solemnly bent over the huge, distorted figure. From top to toe they examined it, not with the eyes of science, but with the authority of men who dealt with the mysteries of life, while the crowd waited with bated breath for their pronouncement. They stood erect, facing each other, and conferred in inaudible tones.

"Wa-al, preachers," demanded an impatient voice, "what conclusion have ye come to? Hey?"

Again, all present recognized that tinder-dry voice

as belonging to David Hannum, banker and horse swapper. The pastors scrambled out of the pit.

"Speak up," insisted Hannum. "Is the critter fish, flesh or good red herrin'?"

"Good people," said one, "we have examined the—ah—body in a spirit of humility and prayerfulness. We have consulted together and have reached accord. There are visible to the naked eye pores such as are present in the human skin. The course of veins and arteries can be traced. The posture indicates—er—that the individual was capable of suffering agony. It is, therefore, our considered opinion—ah—that in this grave, my fellow citizens, lies the veritable petrified—ah—fossilized body of a giant who roamed this earth in biblical days."

A profound sigh arose. Authority had spoken.

There was a commotion in the fringe of the crowd, and a pushing and jostling. An irate voice shouted, "Hey! What's agoin' on here, anyhow? What fur be ye atromplin' my proppity like a herd of wild hawgs?"

It was the owner of the farm, Stubby Newell. Way was made for him to advance to the center, while voices shouted explanations for the trespass:

"Your well diggers struck a stone man! It's a petrified giant out of the Bible! The preachers say so!"

"Hush your noise," growled Stubby, "whilst I see for myself."

He knelt in the earth at the edge of the pit and peered downward. Presently he turned a dumfounded face. "Dawg my cats!" he exclaimed in an awed voice. "Where 'n tunket did this here come from?"

"Brother Newell," said one of the ministers, "only the Almighty knows whence it came. It has been interred here for countless centuries."

"Aw, shucks," Newell said, "some dum fool's playin' off a joke."

"Who'd be able to play sich a joke as this?" asked a neighbor. "Weighs tons. Stands to reason 'tain't no trick, Stubby. It's an honest-to-heaven giant turned to stone, like Lot's wife."

"Salt," said Lossie aloud.

Stubby's unshaven chin was on his breast as he considered this thing that had befallen him. Perhaps it was good fortune, and he needed a bit of luck. All day he had been in Syracuse pleading with adamant bankers for a loan, with no success. He raised his head and his small, closely set, shrewd eyes were gleaming. He had reached a conclusion.

"Wa-al," he said firmly, "whatever it is, it was dug up on my land, so it's mine."

"Nobuddy gainsays that, Stubby."

"Then," he said peremptorily, "all you folks is trespassin'. So skedaddle, the whole passel of ye. Clear out." He waggled a grimy hand at the throng. "From naow on," he announced, "anybuddy that looks at this here wonder of the world pays money fur the privilege." He turned and bowed to the two ministers. "Clergymen half price," he conceded. "Naow, git out, all of ye!"

Growling and grumbling, the crowd withdrew. It was a law-abiding people with a profound respect for the rights of property and a wholesome apprehension of anyone who might have the law on them. Each man guarded his own line fences jealously. This was Stubby Newell's farm, owned in fee simple, and the very Constitution of the United States backed him up when he ordered them off.

Lossie and I were among the last to go because we would have to extricate our horses and buggy. So we watched Stubby as he carried boards from a weathered pile behind his barn and covered the pit with them, hiding from sight that object within, which was to become a national commotion under the name and title of The Cardiff Giant.

The question of whether the thing was human, an ancient work of art or a hoax was to be debated from Maine to California. It was mooted by doctors of divinity, by scientists, by physicians of the eminence of Oliver Wendell Holmes, by college presidents and professors. It was more than a seven days' wonder. It became the subject of a nation-shaking debate in which mysticism, religious awe, esoteric reasoning and ordinary human credulity struggled with logic and science in titanic battle.

Lossie and I drove the few miles to La Fayette and turned down the turnpike toward Syracuse. By this time the Indian Fair was in full swing again, and we drove into the grounds, tied the team and watered it and baited it. Then we sought a shady spot and ate our own lunch. Everywhere the talk was of the find on Stubby Newell's farm. Arguments ran high and noisy, but majority opinion clearly was on the side of petrification of a once-living giant.

Mr. Hannum, who would have seemed naked without his horseman's cap, stopped to speak to Lossie. "Folks," he said in his nasal voice, "air so constituted it's easier to bamboozle 'em than to git 'em to credit a fact."

"Then, sir," I asked, "you think the giant is some kind of a hoax?"

"Didn't say so. Didn't say so," he replied sharply. "More money in it if the's a brisk argymint."

"Money!" I exclaimed.

"I druther own it than have shares in Mr. Vanderbilt's railroad," he said and passed on his way.

It was mid-October and evening came early. We enjoyed the familiar sights of the fair and I bought Lossie an armful of baskets and other things of Indian manufacture. It was nearly five o'clock when we climbed into the buggy and headed for home. Lossie was thoughtful.

"If," she said presently, "that thing is a—a counterfeit, then Stubby Newell didn't think it up."

"Why do you say that?" I asked.

"He's not smart enough, and he couldn't afford it. It would cost a lot of money."

"All the more reason," I argued, "for thinking it genuine."

Then she really shocked me. "I guess I'm an agnostic," she said, looking straight in front of her and wearing an expression of bland innocence.

"Lossie Fox!" I exclaimed, and then, because I did

not know exactly what to say, I said, "Robert Ingersoll is an agnostic."

"He," she said provocatively, "is a very smart man."

"He corrupts people," I said, "going around making fun of the Bible!"

"I looked him up in the dictionary," Lossie said. "I mean I looked up 'agnostic.' I just bet, for all your college, you don't know what it means."

"It means," I said firmly, "a man who doesn't believe in God."

She shook her head. "It's a new word," she said, "and it was coined by a scientist named Huxley, and what it really means is suspending judgment on all matters where there isn't proof of their truth. Mr. Ingersoll doesn't say he doesn't believe in God. He just says there isn't any proof of him. So, about this stone giant I'm an agnostic." She grinned impishly at me. "And that," she said, "isn't all I'm an agnostic about."

"What else?" I asked her.

"That hussy across the street from us," she said. "That Madam Cissie Janeway!"

I growled at her. "You'll get into trouble saying you're an agnostic," I warned. And it was very true. If such a word got around about her, it would be pretty serious—almost as serious as if somebody were to start a scandal that she was a loose woman. She giggled.

* * 2 * *

IT was dark when we turned into our driveway.
It would be past suppertime. "Put up the horses," Lossie
said, "and come on in. I'll get us something to eat."

As I have said, our two families were on the most
intimate terms; so it was proper for me to go in their
kitchen door without knocking. Lossie was setting out
things on the kitchen table. The wood fire was out in the
range, so we made the best of cold meat and bread and
butter and milk and sugar cookies. When we were
through, Lossie dismissed me brusquely, as she had been
wont to do as a child.

"Go on home now," she said. "I'm tired. I want to
go to bed."

I was perfectly willing, and went out of the back
door. I was not tired, but I was disturbed. First I was
disturbed by the change in Lossie. I was disturbed by her
irreverence, which was no new thing. I was disturbed
to find that she was very lovely, and was aware of it.
I was disturbed to discover that her tomboyishness, which
had been all right four or five years ago, had turned into
something that was not tomboyishness, but that showed

many of its qualities, such as daring and independence and a flouting of things that were shibboleths of our everyday life. In short, I was disturbed to perceive that she had become an individual, a young woman of marked character. I was almost on the point of admitting in my thoughts that she had developed into a personage.

I sat down in a rustic chair on our lawn and lighted a corncob pipe, a habit I had acquired in college. The street was dark under its bordering trees. Across the street there was a light in the upstairs front room, which I guessed to be Madam Janeway's bedroom. On the ground floor there was only a dim night light in the vestibule. I was invisible where I sat because it was very dark under our maples. There were many things for me to ponder over and time passed unnoticed. The air was growing chilly and I looked at my watch, which had been a graduation present from father. It was half after ten. I stood up, meaning to go in to bed, when I saw movement across the street in the Janeway yard— stealthy movement.

A dark figure appeared around the side of the house, slinking, bent almost double. Whoever it was had made his way in from the rear. So furtive were the movements of the man that I thought he might be a burglar. And was about to shout a warning and run across the street to frighten him away. But the marauder, if marauder he was, stood huddled against the wall under the library window and whistled a distinctive, quavering bird call. This was strange behavior for a burglar. It might, I reasoned, be some young man seeking a tryst with one of the servants.

After a few moments, I saw a light moving inside the room, and then the side door under the porte-cochere opened silently and a woman stood on the threshold. She stood there sheltering the flame of the lamp from the evening breeze. Its glow illuminated the woman's face. It was Madam Janeway, but her features were not now stately, aristocratic or beautiful. In that brief moment while she was visible, it seemed to me that her emotions were rage and fear. The lurking figure darted up the steps and stood an instant confronting Madam Janeway. Before he pushed past her into the house, I saw his face indistinctly; not so clearly that I could swear to his identity in a court of law. But of one thing I was quite certain, and that was that he wore side whiskers of the sort called sideburns or burnsides. The door closed firmly behind the couple and all was darkness again.

This was a sort of incident our staid neighborhood was not accustomed to. I considered for a moment making further investigation, but then it became apparent to me that it was none of my business. So I went into the house and climbed the stairs to my bedroom. But it was some time before I could get to sleep. I kept thinking of Lossie's remark that she was agnostic on the subject of Madam Janeway.

The country was still staggering from the tragic impact of Black Friday, which had shocked the nation only three weeks ago. Jay Gould and Jim Fisk had plotted to corner gold. It was a scandal that touched the White House, for General Grant's brother-in-law, Corbin, had assured Gould that the Federal Government would not intervene. However, on that day of unrestrained hysteria on the gold exchange, the President had ordered the sale of Treasury gold. The repercussions of that day shook the foundations of financial institutions from coast to coast.

We in Syracuse were sure that hypocritical old Dan'l Drew and Gould and flamboyant Jim Fisk were allied with the powers of darkness, because their enemy Commodore Vanderbilt was an admired friend of ours. Indeed, we had named a city square for him, and we had followed eagerly the struggle between these giants for control of the Erie Railroad.

These men were mythical figures to us, titans moving mysteriously in an alien world—all of them except the Commodore, who had visited us and been seen by us. Many of our more eminent citizens even had shaken his august hand.

These things are matters of history, which you would not think would touch James Street except as a financial convulsion is bound to affect every citizen, rich and poor. But you would have been mistaken, because James Street was touched, modified, shaken and almost destroyed, merely by the strange, the unbelievable use of one of their names. This was the name of the most despicable of that evil triumvirate, old Dan'l Drew.

It was at breakfast on Saturday morning—the day after the discovery of the stone giant on Stubby Newell's farm—that I heard the first whisper of it.

"Banker Watts," my mother said, "is planning a dinner to introduce this Madam Janeway to Syracuse society." And then, "Of course, we shall attend."

"No one will stay away," father said sardonically, "who can walk." He addressed himself to his food for minutes, and then said in a sort of roguish way he had when he was teasing mother, "Of course, you wouldn't have heard the whisper. You wouldn't listen to gossip."

"I notice," mother responded briskly, "that it's you men who always get the first breath of scandal."

"The name of Dan'l Drew came up," said father.

"That sanctimonious old hypocrite!" mother said.

"Well," father told her, "the whisper going around is that Madam Janeway is a protégée of Drew's."

"What kind of a protégée?" mother demanded sharply.

"Not specified," father answered; "but knowing Dan'l's reputation for piety, I'd guess it was platonic."

"Fiddlesticks!" mother snorted. And then, "Who says so?"

"I wouldn't know," father answered. "It's just wafted on the breeze."

Mother sniffed. "Like the ordor of skunk in the autumn," she said rather more inelegantly than was her custom.

When we arose from the table I walked downtown to my small office, in which I was ready to practice law if some client would retain me for that purpose. I had graduated from Mr. Cornell's college in Ithaca and then had read law in the office of Mr. Strangeways to enable me to pass the bar examination, which I did. And then, as was the case with most young lawyers, I wondered what to do next. So I rented a small office, had my name painted on its door and spent my days learning to blow smoke rings. I stood in my window, looking down at the street. Catercorner across the square was Mr. Watts' bank. Directly across was a sort of general store, and as I stood watching, Stubby Newell drove up behind his scrubby-looking team and went in. In a short time, aided by a clerk, he loaded a great bale of canvas in his wagon and drove away.

I occupied myself by reading the morning paper, and then, being a serious young man in whom right principles of diligence and a horror of wasted time had been inculcated, I took down a volume of the Commentaries of the great Chancellor Kent and applied myself to study. It was half past ten by my gold watch when someone rapped on my door and I called an invitation to enter, composing myself to dignified posture and placing the law book where it would be seen by my visitor. It was, to my disappointment, no client, but only Bub Whitty, who was Mr. Watts' office boy.

"He wants to see you over to the bank," Bub said.

"What for?" I asked.

"He didn't say," Bub told me, and backed out of the office.

A young man in my position does not disregard a command from a prominent banker, so I put on my hat and cut across the square. As the door of Mr. Watts' of-

fice was closed, I rapped on it and was bidden to enter.
I stopped suddenly just over the threshold, and I fear I
gawped. For, skirts carefully arranged and one tiny foot
visible and a tiny bonnet perched upon her modishly arranged hair, there was Madam Janeway, sitting beside
the banker's desk. He looked across at me with the aus-
tere dignity befitting a man of his eminence.

"Madam Janeway," he said, "here is the young man
of whom I spoke. Orrin Applegate."

I bowed and was flustered. Madam Janeway smiled
charmingly and extended a hand protected by a lace
mitt. Somehow I felt that I should bow over it and kiss
her fingers. She created that sort of atmosphere.

"How do you do, Mr. Applegate," she said in a rich
contralto voice. "It was gracious of you to come."

"It was a pleasure," I responded, and waited.

Though there was a third chair, Mr. Watts did not
invite me to occupy it. I was not entitled to sit in his
presence.

"Madam Janeway," he said, with a bow in her direction, "retains, of course, eminent counsel to attend to
her larger affairs. But there will be numerous petty details and unimportant matters in which she will require
the services of a local lawyer."

I contented myself by bowing, but I was elated.

"Therefore," Mr. Watts continued in his pompous
way, "I have recommended you to serve in that capacity."

"Thank you, sir," I replied.

"I hope," Madam Janeway said cordially, "that you

will have some time to devote to my affairs."

Mr. Watts sniffed, but I bowed and assured her that I would be at her service.

"I suggested to Mr. Watts," she said, "that we have some arrangement on a——" She hesitated for the word.

"Retainer basis," said Mr. Watts. "I told her you would be glad of fifty dollars monthly."

I resented his manner and words—a successful man patronizing and belittling a youngster just starting his professional career. Madam Janeway lifted her brows as if she, too, were displeased.

"It will be satisfactory," I said gravely. It would, indeed, be satisfactory. Fifty dollars a month represented a substantial income.

"That will be all then, Orrin," Mr. Watts said abruptly. "When Madam has an errand for you, she will send for you."

I was taking an intense dislike to Mr. Watts, and this curt dismissal frayed my temper. But Madam Janeway smiled so delightfully, and so plainly let me see that she understood my resentment that I bowed politely before withdrawing.

"Please don't go, Mr. Applegate," she said. "We must become acquainted. If Mr. Watts wishes to be rid of us——" She gave him an arch smile, and he purred.

"Indeed not, Madam Janeway," he hastened to say. "Remain as long as you like." He turned to me. "Perhaps you'd better sit down, Orrin."

I preferred to stand.

"I think," he said in an instant, "that Madam Janeway wishes to ask you about what happened at the Newell farm yesterday. I understand you were present. It seems to have reached her ears."

"It seems," she said, and her tone was almost a rebuke, "to have reached many ears. What are the facts, Mr. Applegate?"

"While digging a well," I said cautiously, "workmen discovered a great stone figure. A gigantic figure. Two clergymen who were present declared it to be the petrified body of a once-living titan."

"How strange! How unbelievable! And what, Mr. Applegate, is your own opinion?"

I almost repeated Lossie's word—that on this matter I was agnostic. But discretion halted me. "I have reserved judgment," I said.

"As a professional man naturally would do," she said. "May one see this marvel?"

"My guess," said I, "is that Stubby Newell plans to exhibit it for a fee. I think I saw him loading a tent on his wagon this morning."

"I'm interested in antiquities." Again she gave me the full force of her charming smile. "Oh, I'm remiss," she said, fumbling in her reticule and bringing out a roll of currency. From it she separated a fifty-dollar note and extended it to me. Again she smiled not as a client, but as a contemporary, and with mischievous humor. "I wonder, Mr. Applegate, if this retainer will include extralegal courtesies."

"Certainly, Madam Janeway," I told her. "How

may I serve you?"

"I'm unfamiliar with the country," she said. "I wonder if you can dine with me and then drive out to this place with me. To show my coachman the way. I simply must see this astonishing thing!"

"I shall be happy to do so," I assured her.

She rose, bowed prettily to Mr. Watts and took my arm. We left the bank and I handed her into her carriage, taking my seat beside her. We drove out to her home and I assisted her to alight under the porte-cochere. She opened the door and preceded me into the parlor, where she motioned me to a seat on the haircloth sofa. Excusing herself, she left me alone. Presently the butler came in and asked if I would care for a drink of liquor. Naturally, I declined, and he bowed stiffly. He was a strange-looking creature, very tall, pallid, skeletal of figure and with a face like a death's head, in which burned the blackest eyes I ever had seen. He turned and walked out of the room as silently as a cat. As he turned his back it was apparent that, in spite of his emaciation, he had shoulders of surprising width. When he reached the door he paused, turned his head over his shoulder and stared at me fixedly. It was startling. Then he disappeared.

Madam Janeway and I dined together. It was not the heavy noonday meal to which I was accustomed, but more on the dainty side. When we had finished, she rang for the butler, calling him Oscar, and bade him summon her carriage. In a minute or so he reappeared to tell her the carriage was waiting. We went out and took our seats and were driven into James Street. As we turned into the public road, I saw Lossie in a hammock on her lawn. At sight of me beside Madam Janeway, she straightened so suddenly that she all but fell out. The last I saw of her as we trotted up the street was laughable. She was standing, bent a little forward, with her mouth agape. I chuckled.

"What is it?" Madam asked.

"Nothing. Nothing," I answered.

"She is a lovely child," said Madam demurely.

We followed the turnpike to the intersection which led to Cardiff, and presently took the rougher side road down the valley to Stubby's farm. We were not alone. Many rigs were heading for the same destination, and when we arrived at the farm there were a score of people standing in line waiting for admission to the tent which Stubby had erected over the pit in which lay the giant. There was even a ticket booth stating that admission was fifty cents. Madam produced a dollar and I procured tickets, and we took our places in the queue. In ten minutes we were leaning on the rail which Stubby had erected around the hole and staring down at that strange, bewildering, distorted figure, so grotesquely human in the dim light under the canvas.

Madam gazed down at it for a long time, and then turned to me with a serious face. "It is a marvel," she said in a hushed voice. "That noble expression must once have expressed the character of a leader among men. I have seen enough." Then she said an odd thing. "I should like to see this man Newell," she told me.

"He must be worth observing."

"There he stands," I said, pointing.

She stared at him fixedly and shook her head. "Not that man!" she exclaimed. "There must be someone behind him."

This I did not comprehend, nor did I think it polite to ask her meaning. We re-entered the carriage and drove back to town. I saw her up the steps and took my departure. No one was visible on our side as I crossed the street, but no sooner had I reached the path to our door than Lossie popped around the corner of the house and confronted me, hands on slender hips and fire in her eyes. She said no word, but stepped close to me and then, without warning, slapped my face so vigorously that I staggered; and, turning, ran as fast as she could for her own kitchen door.

My cheek tingled as I stood staring after her, but I was not enraged. If I could have caught her, I would undoubtedly have smacked her, as had happened years ago when we quarreled. I was not angry, but on the contrary and to my own astonishment, I was pleased. I even laughed with genuine amusement. It was the last time I was to be amused by anything for a long time to come.

I awakened early on a beautiful Sunday morning and went downstairs to buckwheat cakes and maple syrup. I had put on my new black suit, and my beaver hat was carefully brushed. Father and mother and I would go to church, of course, and then the Foxes were to have dinner with us, as it was our turn. Next Sunday we would eat with them. In fine weather we always walked to church—both families in a sort of solemn parade.

Father and I strolled out to see to the horses. I threw open the big barn doors to give light. I went to the oat bin while father went to the stalls, and I heard him utter a strangled noise, as if someone had punched him in the stomach. I dropped the scoop and went to where he stood, frozen, staring into our carriage. From his very position I could sense that something was wrong —something was very wrong. On the rear seat of our carriage sat a stranger, leaning back against the cushion, but with his head on his breast. He was a bearded man with the sort of whiskers named after General Burnside. From between his teeth, horribly, protruded a swollen tongue; his heavy face was livid and he was unmistakably dead. He had been strangled.

* * 3 * *

W HO," demanded my father, "put that thing in my barn?" He was, it seemed, not so much startled or alarmed as outraged that anyone would commit such a nuisance upon his property. His mustache bristled. His second reaction was more dynamic. "Great Scot!" he said loudly. "The man has been murdered." He turned upon me as if I were somehow to blame. "You," he commanded, "go fetch an officer of the law to get it out of here! Scamper!"

I scampered, fully aware that officers of the law would not be so easily come by in our orderly city at such an hour on the Sabbath morning. As I ran down the street I heard father bellowing, "Hey, Lander! Come out here, Lander! There's a damn corpse in my barn!"

Lander was, of course, Lossie's father, Mr. Leander Fox, and it was natural for father to call for him in any emergency. All their lives they had done things together —played together as children, striven together as young men and shared good and ill as partners. What touched one of them touched both. I knew that Mr. Fox would come running at the urgency in father's voice, running as fast as his short, pudgy legs would carry his short, stubby body.

I called him Uncle Lander as Lossie called my father Uncle Silas, though, of course, there was no blood relationship. As I made for the street I heard the side screen door burst open and Uncle Lander's voice demand, "What in tunket's the matter, Silas? What you shouting for?"

A few months ago it would have been difficult to locate an officer, but only recently the state legislature had passed a bill authorizing us to hire additional police-men. It was not dignified for a young attorney at law to run, but I walked rapidly to Salina Street, where I saw a patrolman sauntering along placidly. He was a middle-aged and whiskered man, who blinked at me as I accosted him excitedly.

"Now hold your hosses, bub," he admonished. "Who be ye and what ails ye?"

"I'm Orrin Applegate," I told him, "and there's a murdered man in our barn."

"Applegate, huh?" he asked, becoming more re-spectful at mention of father's name. "Murdered man, ye say?"

"Dead," I said impressively.

Clearly he did not know what to do next. "I'm just a peeler," he said. "Murders is too steep fur me. "I'll mosey along to your house, but you better fetch somebuddy higher up."

So he set off—reluctantly, I thought—while I

hurried on to the home of the commissioner and rang his bell. He was arrayed for church, but he told his family to go on without him. As he walked toward James Street he questioned me, but there was little I could tell him. He was uncomfortable, being a business-man newly appointed, and no trained policeman. In our yard, when we arrived, a knot of neighbors was milling about. Father saw us and advanced toward us belligerently.

He spoke testily to the commissioner. "This police-man of yours," he said loudly, "hasn't got the sense God gave geese. He does nothing but gawk. Look, Sam, I don't want my property cluttered up with corpses on a Sunday morning. Haul it away from here, Sam."

"Now, Applegate," the commissioner said placat-ingly, "just hold your hosses. Don't blame you for being put out, but if there's been a murder, it's got to be looked into thorough. Who is it got murdered?"

"How the devil would I know?" father said. "All I want is to get him out of my carriage and off my premises."

"We'll have to look at him," said the commissioner, and the ensuing proceedings were highly informal. He invited the neighbors into the barn to take a look and see if they could identify the victim. No one ever had seen the man before.

"Maybe," suggested Uncle Lander, "there's suthin' in his pockets to tell who he is."

It was quite evident the commissioner was reluctant to make the gruesome search. He ordered the patrolman to undertake the unpleasant task, but nothing came to light. The man's pockets had been emptied.

"Beats all," said the frustrated commissioner. "How we ever going to find out who he is?"

Uncle Lander had a sense of humor, not always held properly in check. It was a defect Lossie had come by through inheritance. "Wa-al," he said in his high, crisp voice, "you might lay him out in state in the city hall and have everybody file past him."

Other policemen arrived—professionals who went about their business somewhat more efficiently, but with no results. No clue came to light. So, presently, the body was carted away to a downtown funeral parlor, we having no morgue at that time. The people who had been trampling our grass withdrew and the two families were left alone. As Lossie's father said, "All dressed up and no place to go."

We sat on our porch, stiff and uncomfortable, for it was a warm morning. I was more uncomfortable than anyone else because I was worried. I admit I am slow to reach decisions, and cautious, as is proper for a young man trained in the law. I was not sure I had acted correctly in keeping to myself the fact that I had seen a man with sideburn whiskers calling stealthily upon Madam Janeway. But quite definitely I could not swear to the fact that our dead man and Madam's visitor were one and the same. If I spoke of this to the police, it would undoubtedly offend Madam Janeway, and I had been reared among people who were reluctant to give offense to neighbors. In addition to this, Madam Janeway was a client of mine, my first real client, and I was not certain of the ethics of the situation. Moreover, Madam Janeway was a wealthy lady, aristocratic, with high connections. It was unthinkable that such an individual could have any guilty connection with the killing of a man. I reached the conclusion that I was quite justified in keeping my mouth shut.

I was conscious that Lossie was leaning forward and staring at me with alert, bright eyes. She got up and came to sit in the chair beside me and continued to stare at close range.

She leaned toward me and spoke in a whisper. "You might as well tell me now," she said. "You know I'll get it out of you."

"Tell you what?" I asked uncomfortably.

"What you know about this murder," she said.

"I know nothing about it," I said firmly.

"Orrin Applegate," she said, "you're talking to Lossie. Remember Lossie? Well, she knows you from *A* to izzard." She wrinkled her nose at me. "Maybe," she said, "you can keep a secret, but you never could and never will be able to keep it a secret that you have a secret. You might as well tell me one time as another."

"You think yourself very smart," I said angrily.

"And so I am," she said complacently. "I'm smarter than Roscoe Conkling and Charles Sumner rolled into one—plus a woman's intuition."

I would never admit it to her, but I agreed that it was so. She was a steel trap for smartness. It was not decorous for a girl to be so smart, and I resented it.

But her attack upon me was interrupted. Across the steet we saw Madam Janeway's handsome span of horses bring her carriage from the barn to stop beneath the porte-cochere. The lady came out of the door and tripped down the steps to take her seat with languid grace. She put up a tiny, modish parasol and held it elegantly over her head. The carriage debouched upon the street and went away at a spanking pace. Madam did not so much as glance in our direction. She was a picture of reserved aristocracy and dignity.

Lossie sniffed. "Attorney Applegate's client!" she said quite nastily. And then, "We never had any murders on this block till she moved here."

"Lossie Fox!" exclaimed her mother chidingly.

"A buzzard," Lossie said unheedingly, "in peacock's clothing."

"You," I said sharply, "should be ashamed of yourself."

"And you," she said, "ought to go out to an Indian medicine man and buy you an amulet to ward off spells and incantations."

"I thought you children were grown up," my mother said, with disapproval of our bickering.

"I am," Lossie said, having the last word.

We sat, the two families, on our front porch. Our fathers speculated about the murder, which annoyed more than it alarmed them. It never occurred to either that it could be more than a nuisance to my father or that the finding of a corpse in his barn could throw the slightest suspicion upon him. Or that, now the body had been removed to the funeral parlor, any further embarrassment could touch him. It was a typical attitude. He was Silas Applegate, which meant something in our community. That any wagging tongue should cast any suspicion upon him would amount to lese majesty.

Our mothers found a more interesting topic in Madam Janeway.

"I wonder what church she belongs to," Mrs. Fox said.

"Probably she's a Baptist," my mother guessed. "Our nicest people go the Baptist Church."

"You'll find out she's an atheist," Lossie said disagreeably.

"Oh, no," expostulated her mother. "No lady would be that—especially coming to a new town to live. She wouldn't be received."

"Now, mamma," said the reedy voice of Uncle Lander, "that's nonsense. If she's got money and connections and wears her bustle in the right place, she'd be received if she was a Hottentot." He turned to father. "You get around downtown more than I do. How did this yarn spread that she's some bigwig's fancy woman?"

"That version I haven't heard," father replied. "But I've heard Dan'l Drew's name mentioned."

"Anyhow," said Mr. Fox, "Banker Watts' dinner and reception for her is going to be the event of the year."

"I know somebody who won't go to it," I said with malicious intent.

"Whom do you mean, Orrin?" my mother asked.

"Lossie," I said, and grinned my most sarcastic grin at her.

"Don't be stupid," she retorted. "Of course I'll go if I'm invited. And if I'm not invited I'll crawl in through the kitchen window."

I snorted. "You'll be more likely to hang around outside and steal the pies," I told her. This was a reference to a crime suggested by her and committed by both of us not too long ago, when we had done a similar depredation against a Congregational chicken-pie sociable.

Church had let out by this time and neighbors stopped in on their way home, and several people who were not neighbors, but had gone quite out of their way to satisfy curiosity. Among these were good friends whose concern and sympathy at the day's tragic event was sincere and genuine, but there were others who came hopeful that they might collect some morsel of gossip, or find our family alarmed or shaken, or even that we had somehow been smirched by it. Everywhere, but especially in little cities like ours, there are characters like that, jealous of decent social position and integrity, and avid to hear and to repeat some malicious talk. It was not difficult to separate the sheep from the goats and my mother was amply able to deal with the situation. Mother could be formidable.

Our cook rang the dinner bell. No matter what casual guests might be there, Libby was not going to have her dinner spoiled. The last of the callers took hasty departure and we filed into the dining room, where father sat at the head of the table, mother at the foot, Uncle Lander and his wife at one side, and Lossie and I elbow to elbow. Father asked a blessing in which he gave God directions as to how to run the world for the next week. Then, precipitately, he commenced to serve fricasseed chicken and biscuits and rich yellow gravy and mashed potatoes, all heaped upon each plate.

I watched Lossie out of the corner of my eye to see what new tricks of dining etiquette she might have picked up in Europe. But foreign travel seemed not to have affected her appetite. Always, even at her most tomboyish, she had been dainty and somehow fastidious —if you can imagine a fastidious tomboy. She was even slenderer and daintier now. She looked, I thought, as if she lived on a diet of hummingbirds' tongues. But in one thing she had not changed. She loved food. She tucked away that dinner as if she were a canawler after a hard trip.

After her second helping had been disposed of, and a section of pumpkin pie, I whispered to her, "Keep on gormandizing like that and in ten years you'll be fatter than Aunt Lizzie."

She wrinkled her nose at me. "Don't you worry, Mr. Applegate," she answered. "What I eat doesn't go to fat. I need a lot to feed my brain."

I studied her openly and was bewildered. "Lossie Fox," I said crossly, "you look like a fairy princess, but you act like a lock tender on the Erie Canal."

Lossie used a favorite expression of her mother's

signifying a person lacking in something desirable. It might be initiative; it might be a sense of humor; it might be liveliness or intelligence. It was an all-around handy phrase to express disapproval.

"Orrin," Lossie retorted, "you look like a Don Juan, but you're nothing but a stick-in-the-mud."

Father and Uncle Lander, as always after a Sunday dinner, were replete and sleepy. They retired to father's study and presently were snoring. Our mothers went upstairs, possibly to avoid being seen to nod inelegantly. Lossie was wide awake.

"Let's walk down to the canal," she said. Walking was an amusement that could be indulged in on the Sabbath without criticism, so Lossie and I set out in a leisurely way toward the canal, where we could stand clear of the towpath and watch the boats go by. On the way we passed the large, nondescript brick house of Mr. Vivus Smith, a political friend of Thurlow Weed and Horace Greeley. Indeed it was claimed that the Republican Party was born there at a conference among the three. We trudged on to the weigh lock and stood on the bridge over the towpath, which climbed and dipped in a manner that must have been discouraging to the horses.

We loitered there in the sunshine and then strolled along to the packet dock, for it was time for the passenger packet to arrive from the east. A small crowd was congregated to meet expected arrivals, some standing on the street-level sidewalk above the water, others crowded on the narrow dock. Lossie and I leaned over the wall to watch.

The packet, painted and elegant, and crowded with excursionists and with travelers with westward destinations, approached sedately up the canal, its upper deck with its long benches crowded with passengers, jostled the wall of the canal and came to rest.

A good half of the passengers scrambled ashore, but the packet did not cast off. There was some turmoil and Lossie and I saw members of the crew assisting in the effort to get from the rear deck to the shore a large wagon, a sort of van, ornately painted and gilded. With shouts and profanity the thing was run across planks to the towpath and there a team of horses were attached to it. And then, issuing from the cabin of the canal boat, came a strange assortment of people.

Ahead waddled an impossibly fat woman. Trotting at her side was a tiny manikin wearing a tall beaver hat. Behind them marched a man in Zouave costume who led an enormous cinnamon bear by a ring in his nose. Then came a slender young woman who, from where we stood, seemed young and beautiful. She clung to the arm of one of the handsomest men I ever have seen. He was dressed more elegantly and expensively than you would have expected a member of such a troupe to be. In addition to a tall beaver hat, he carried a gold-headed cane. It was evident from his manner of giving orders that he was the owner or manager of the group. Bringing up the rear, strutted a tall, cadaverous man in somber black, dragging by the hand a small, pale boy.

This procession made its way to the street. Apparently it knew where it was going because there was no hesitation or questioning as it headed down the street and disappeared around the next corner.

"We," said I ironically, "are going to have some tony entertainment." All the same, I was a little excited, because performances of any sort were few and far between. This, if I was not mistaken, would be a free show whose purpose was to attract a crowd to whom to sell patent medicine of some sort.

Lossie was frowning, eyes puckered as she concentrated upon some problem. "That handsome man," she said in a queer tone. "I've seen him somewhere—or his picture—and it wasn't in a show." She shook her head. "I don't know why," she went on slowly, "but it surprised me to see him in such company."

"Aw, shucks!" I said. "You're just struck in a heap because he is so handsome. Probably you'll be getting infatuated with him and eloping, like girls in paper-backed novels."

She made no retort, which was unusual, and I felt her shiver, though the afternoon was still warm.

"Please take me home, Orrin," she said. "I want to be safe at home."

When you come to think of it, it was strange that the petrified giant out at Cardiff should cause so much more public interest and excitement than the finding of the body of a murdered man in our barn. But it was so. The Cardiff thing caused a minor madness. People poured into Syracuse by train and canalboat and horse-driven vehicle, so that our hotels were crowded as never before and there was a constant procession of curious visitors going to and coming from Stubby Newell's farm. In the beginning he had charged fifty cents to go into the tent and stare down at the mystery. But right soon he raised the admission fee to a dollar. I chanced to be there when the change was made. It was on the suggestion of the cigar manufacturer, George Hull, but it seemed to me it was more an order than a suggestion.

I compared notes with other visitors and we estimated that Stubby was becoming a rich man by leaps and bounds, for our calculations made us believe that he was taking in an average of twenty-six dollars an hour seven days a week. Stubby had become a showman, aping the great Mr. Barnum in striped trousers and a cutaway coat over a boiled shirt. He was putting on airs. After a few days he added to his importance by delivering a brief lecture describing how the monster had been discovered, and fell in love with the sound of his own voice. The lecture was expanded. It became pious, and it was a treat to listen to Stubby tell how he had been led to make the discovery by the hand of God. It became a matter of divine revelation.

Lossie's father accompanied us to the tent and listened with rapt face to this new revelation. Lossie inherits her disposition to irreverence from Uncle Lander. At the end of Stubby's remarks—which had become a sermon—he cleared his throat in a dry way he had when he was about to give off with some outrageous saying, and remarked loudly, "Beats all how Divine

Providence picked out Stubby to make a prophet out of, don't it? Seems as though the only tool He could have used to rake up Stubby would be a fine-tooth comb."

Now, the purpose of a fine-tooth comb, especially by canawlers and such people, was unpleasantly familiar, and Uncle Lander's remark was much criticized by the religious because it intimated impiously that the Supreme Being would so demean himself as to use a delousing implement.

It was due, of course, to newspaper enterprise that the Cardiff Giant was so widely advertised. The murder was a local thing and not calculated by our editors to be of interest beyond our limits, but the giant was a cat of another color. Accounts of it were telegraphed to New York and Boston, for our two papers used the wires to disseminate news and to receive dispatches from a distance. It was a joint undertaking, because expensive. The telegraph company charged all of four dollars and a half for an hour's use of their facilities. But when that hour was up, even if the Czar of Russia were drowned in the Erie Canal, no word of it could be sent out until the next day.

But to people of our class the absorbing topic was the dinner and reception to be given by Banker Watts to introduce Madam Janeway to Syracuse society. Some twenty of our most prominent citizens were bidden to dine in the Watts' spacious dining room. After which the reception was to be held and scores of people, carefully selected, of course, would form in line and pass the spot between the folding doors where Mr. and Mrs.

Watts would stand with Madam between them. And each passer would be allowed to speak a sentence to the lady in whose honor the select occasion was being held.

Lossie and I, naturally, were not invited to the dinner, but we were permitted to attend the reception. I had no desire to attend, but Lossie was bound and determined.

"You will come for me," she commanded, "by eight o'clock at least."

"They won't be through dinner," I protested.

"Of course not," she said impatiently, "but we'll be watching through the front window, and the minute they get up from the table, we'll scoot over."

"Good," said I. "Then we can come home good and early."

She turned up her nose at me. "We'll stay," she said inelegantly, "till the last dog is hung."

"But why, Lossie? You make out that you despise Madam Janeway. And you throw out nasty hints about her. I shouldn't think you would demean yourself by going at all, much less staying the whole evening."

Lossie giggled. "She'll have such fine manners and elegant deportment that I want to improve myself by studying her," she said. "Besides," she went on demurely, "I want to be sure she notices me. A poor little colorless mousie like me!"

Well, when I walked across the lawn to call for her at eight o'clock, she was no colorless mousie. She wore a gown I never had seen before, and which I accused her of buying for the event. This she did not deny. It fitted tightly above the waist, but from the hips downward it flared and billowed over hoop-skirts with panniers and flounces. And it was an off kind of blue that somehow made you very conscious of her blue eyes. She was elegant—very elegant—and dignified and grown-up and reserved. And most startlingly lovely. Tonight there was nothing of the tomboy about her, and I was taken aback and flustered, and conscious of my awkwardness and ignorance of modish things and ways.

"Gosh all fishhooks!" I exclaimed loutishly.

She stared at me with elevated brows. "If that," she said, "is a compliment, I'm obliged to you, sir. However, it might have been phrased a bit more elegantly."

"I'm not elegant," I said miserably. "I haven't been to Europe to learn how. I haven't learned how to lord it over my old friends and make them feel ashamed of their back-country clumsiness!"

She showed no remorse, nor did any twinkle come into her eyes to hint that she was teasing me. She was very haughty and hoity-toity, and, it seemed to me, vain and frivolous, with a heartless social enamel covering her as a shell covers the meat of a nut.

"If," she said loftily, "there should be dancing, try not to step on my feet."

After all, there is such a thing as self-respect, and even though she was Lossie and my old playmate and chum, there was a point beyond which I could not endure.

47

"Good night, Miss Lossie," I said tightly. "In the future I hope you find a more suitable escort."

"Oh," she said, "I shall do that, of course. But to-night you're all I've got. Come back here, Orrin Applegate!" Then, with a lightning change, she became the Lossie of half a dozen years ago—a tomboy with grimy hands and holes in the knees of her stockings. She lifted her stately skirt so that she could kick, and she did kick me on the shin. "You big clodhopper," she said, "if you get mad at me and don't take me to this party, I'll scratch both your eyes out and step on them."

Somehow, this made everything different. Here was a Lossie I was familiar with, and with whom I knew how to cope.

"Then," I said stoutly, "keep a polite tongue in your head."

She thrust out the tip of a pink tongue. "Ninny-hammer!" she said, and then grabbed me by the arm and steered me to the front door. There she stopped.

"Keep your eyes open this night," she said exultantly. "You will see what you will see."

"And what shall I see?" I demanded.

"You will see," she said, "this Madam Janeway creating a sensation. But you'll see something else, sir. You'll see Lossie Fox creating a sensation, and I'll bet you a cooky mine is the greatest. Come along."

We scurried across the street and down the other side to Banker Watts' square red brick house. As we passed Madam's house, there stood on the lawn near the walk that butler whom I had met when I lunched with

Madam on the day we drove to Cardiff. The man had bulging, bald temples, and eyes recessed in deep hollows, and a mouth of extraordinary width, with lips so thin there seemed to be no lips at all. His nose was a small thing, tilted upward so that one looked directly into his nostrils, and his ears might have been used for fans. A strange, unwholesome creature.

$* \quad * \quad 4 \quad * \quad *$

WE were admitted to Banker Watts' home and
shown directly to where the host and hostess received,
with Madam Janeway, regal, between them. A line was
already forming. As we walked the few steps, I was
conscious that something was happening to Lossie. I
felt a slight movement, a sort of drawing together of
her slender body, a straightening of her shoulders and a
lifting of her chin. She moved a little away from me and
I stared at her. For there had been a transformation. She
no longer was the lovely, tempestuous girl who so
recently had kicked my shin. This person who walked
beside me never had done anything so undignified. She
seemed taller, and somehow she had contrived to seem
more mature. Her very face had altered. It was not pert
with promise of rich beauty to come; it was dignified
by beauty that had amply arrived. It was not a cold,
standoffish beauty, but vivid and arresting and somehow
seductive. Here was nothing naïve, but all the allure of
Eve, who had learned wisdom from the serpent. I did
not like it.

For an instant Mrs. Watts did not recognize Lossie,

and then her pale blue eyes widened and I thought she was going to exclaim, "Well!" But she recovered herself.

"Madam Janeway," she did say, "this is our little neighbor, Lossie Fox."

I got the idea that the older woman was trying to belittle Lossie, but she had no luck whatever. Madam and the girl looked into each other's eyes for an instant, and then both smiled brightly.

"But, my dear!" exclaimed Madam with generous warmth, "I had no idea I had such a beauty for a neighbor!"

"Madam is kind," Lossie said with perfect poise. "But she can well afford to pay a nice compliment. For who could compete with Madam's loveliness?" Her frank eyes swept the woman's figure from top to toe. "And Madam's gown!" Lossie exclaimed. "We do not often see such elegance in our little city!"

Madam Janeway's smile was condescendingly regal as she touched Lossie with her fan. "And your gown, Miss Lossie," she said, "was not created in Syracuse. It fairly reeks of the Rue de la Paix."

With the restless line behind us, we could not linger. Before we passed on, Madam Janeway greeted me with a nicely jocular familiarity. "And my legal adviser!" she said. "How kind of you to come to this reception!"

I led Lossie away, and when we were at a safe distance I said in an angry whisper, "What got into you, Lossie? An hour ago you were going to put poison in her soup. And now butter wouldn't melt in your mouth."

She looked up at me and her lip curled slightly. Her

shining eyes were enigmatic. "Madame Janeway," she said, "is exquisite. One has but to see her to lose one's heart! Such glamour!"

"Come off it, Loss," I said testily. "What are you up to?"

"Oh, Orrin," she said girlishly, although her eyes were not girlish, but sardonic. "I want to study Madam, to pattern myself after her. To learn decorum." She was all but cooing in a sickening manner.

"You wouldn't," I snapped, "pattern yourself after the Queen of Sheba!"

"Who was," Lossie said softly, "a very astute lady. Who," she went on with lifted brows, "bamboozled the wisest man who ever lived. Maybe Madam has taken a leaf out of Sheba's book."

The formal part of the reception came to an end. With half an eye one could see that Madam Janeway had scored a triumph. Syracuse would be at her feet. But something else I saw with much less pleasure. Lossie was scoring no mean triumph herself. Men old enough to be her grandfather gathered about her, palavering. Young men drooled at the mouth. Now, I'm somewhat shy by nature and not a pushing sort of person, so I found myself in the background. Not that I cared very much. Not that Lossie playing the coquette to perfection meant anything to me. But I do not like to be kidded, especially by a miss who had tagged after me from babyhood. She was showing off. All right. I was only Orrin Applegate, drab and sober, not handsome nor witty, but I had too much pride to let her see that I was annoyed. Certainly I was not jealous.

Lossie seemed wholly unaware of me, as she was the center of an eager group—a group, if truth must be told, that was as large as that surrounding Madam Janeway. I joined the circle paying homage to the older woman, and she smiled at me graciously and drew me into the conversation with older men who, I was conscious, regarded me as only a boy. But Madam was gracious, tapping me with her fan.

"I've great confidence in Mr. Applegate," she said so that all might hear. "He is to handle my legal affairs. I find him very astute in such matters."

That changed the attitude of the group materially, and more than one of them eyed me with some envy, for it is a very desirable thing to be legal advisor to so wealthy and highly connected a person as Madam Janeway. Mr. Watts pushed his way to her side, accompanied by a stranger, a man with lofty forehead, shrewd eyes, hair that covered the upper half of his ears. He was wearing a black stock with a jeweled pin, and his manner seemed a bit pompous, though not disagreeably so.

"Madam Janeway," Mr. Watts said, "may I present a gentleman newly arrived from New York whose name may not be wholly unknown to you—Mr. Phineas T. Barnum?"

"Indeed I know the name of Mr. Barnum. We are grateful to him for bringing to us the exquisite voice of Jenny Lind," she exclaimed.

"And the less exquisite voice of General Tom Thumb," the great showman answered with a broad grin.

"And what, sir, brings you to our little city?" Madam asked.

"Curiosity, ma'am. A hint of the strange and marvelous. Where the seemingly miraculous manifests itself, there you will find P. T. Barnum. If it is something people will pay to see—then, ma'am, I must be the one to exhibit it. I suffer no rivals, ma'am. If the world wants to see or hear or to admire a thing, then it must come to my museum to marvel at it."

Madam had guessed immediately the reason for Mr. Barnum's presence in Syracuse.

"Of course," she said agreeably. "Naturally, you will have come to investigate the Cardiff Giant."

"That is indeed so. Have you seen the monster, ma'am?"

"In all its mysterious glory," she smiled.

"And your opinion, ma'am, if I may make so bold as to ask?"

"In your skilled hands, Mr. Barnum, it can become a wonder of the world. Actually, even in lesser hands, it bids fair to create a furor."

"In the morning," Mr. Barnum said in his pompous way, "I shall proceed to the spot to see with my own eyes."

"Sir," said Madam simply, "it will pleasure me to drive you to the spot. My attorney, Mr. Applegate, will, I'm quite sure, accompany us." She raised her brows at me inquiringly.

"I shall be delighted," I assured her.

I went presently to see if I could extricate Lossie

from her admirers. As I wormed my way across the room I contrived to displace a handsomely bound small Bible from its place on a marble-topped table. It fell face downward and open. A gentleman at my side stooped to pick it up, and as he did so he examined it, and then he emitted a low whistle.

"Cast an eye over this," he said to me, and showed me the blank page at the front of the book. On it was an inscription in crabbed handwriting. There were few words, but they were sufficent to create a furor that would almost equal that about the Cardiff Giant. The written words were:

"To my little Cissie, with the affection of Uncle Daniel Drew."

How characteristic it was that that sanctimonious old hypocrite should give to his niece, or his mistress, or his illegitimate daughter a copy of Holy Writ.

Although Lossie was enjoying herself greatly, and, to my mind, acting somewhat giddy about all the admiration she was attracting, we had to leave the reception with our parents. We approached Madam Janeway to say good night, and never did you see such cordiality as was shown by the two of them. I was nonplused. Lossie, who had been so vehemently hostile to Madam, was close to being effusive now. Madam, whom you might have expected to show some petulance because Lossie had shone so brilliantly at the reception which had been exclusively in her honor, behaved toward Lossie as if she were vastly proud of her and gratified by it all. How is one to know when women are being straightforward and when they are contriving and guileful?

"Good night, my dear Miss Fox," Madam said, and smiled gaily. "Why should I not call you Lossie when we are such close neighbors and, I hope, destined to be close friends?"

"I'd love it, Madam Janeway," Lossie responded, purring with pleasure like a stroked kitten.

"And," said the older woman, "it would be charming if you called me Madam Cissie. We mustn't be formal. And by the way, Lossie, we—Mr. Applegate and I—are driving the great Mr. Barnum out to Cardiff in the morning to show him the eighth wonder of the world. It would be lovely if you would accompany us."

"Oh, Madam Cissie," Lossie gushed, "I'd love it! I'd love it!"

We extricated ourselves and followed our parents down the street. Our fathers walked side by side and our mothers behind them so they could discuss Madam Janeway in a strictly feminine manner, without masculine ears to overhear. Lossie and I lagged behind.

"Well," I said unpleasantly, "you did make a giddy spectacle of yourself!"

She was walking on air. "Tomorrow," she said gleefully, "I'll be the talk of the town. You'll see. Didn't I tell you? What'll you bet I'm not sent a dozen bouquets of flowers tomorrow?"

"None from me," I said. "You're a snip. A vain little snip."

She did not flare up as I had expected, but laughed a

rippling little laugh. "But a much admired little snip," she retorted.

"And," I went on, "you wriggled and rubbed against Madam Janeway like a puppy dog."

"Now did I?" she asked. "And what about Madam Cissie? She wriggled back, didn't she?" She paused a second, and then laughed again and said, "Madam is a very, very smart woman. We're going to be such friends!"

Well, there it was, and how was I, a commonplace young man, to cope with it? Lossie blew hot and she blow cold. One moment she was a society belle and the next she was a hoyden. One minute she hated and the next moment she doted. But in one particular she was consistent, never varying, and it did not make me happy. She flouted me always, and treated me as of no particular account, and used me as some handy object, to be given no thought or consideration; only to be used at need and then to be ignored.

She crowed. "Oh, Orrin!" she cried. "It's wonderful, gorgeous, to grow up!" And then she turned a pert, impudent face up to me and asked mischievously, "Why don't you try it?"

I could have shaken her, and came close to it.

"Don't pout," she said. "It's not becoming in a member of the bar."

I was glad to leave her at her door and to cut across the lawn to our house. I undressed quickly and lay awake in the darkness, thinking about Lossie and Madam Janeway and what was to come of it all, until I fell asleep and did not awaken until father's voice called me at six o'clock the next morning.

After breakfast I stood under Lossie's window and called "Yoo-hoo," and she flung up the sash and scolded me for it, pointing out that I was a hobbledehoy and had no manners, and that a gentleman did not stand under a window and yoo-hoo for a lady.

"I've yoo-hooed for you since you were a year old," I answered, "and I don't propose to stop."

She leaned over the window sill, lovely as a flower, and there was another of those breath-taking changes in her mood. She smiled down wistfully. "Please, please, Orrin," she said softly, "never stop calling. Never. Never."

She came down shortly and we crossed the street to Madam's and sat in her cool parlor until she came down, stately and beautiful and smiling with anticipation. We got into her carriage and drove to the hotel for the great man, and then headed out the avenue toward Cardiff. There was no need for us to talk; Mr. Barnum did that. He did not converse as an ordinary man or in common language. He spoke in superlatives, and such naïve vanity I never have beheld. Nothing was ordinary; everything was "prodigious" or "beyond belief" or "awesome." His famous elephant, Jumbo, was not an elephant; it was a "ponderous, palm-eared, pea-eyed pachyderm." I could feel Lossie, on the seat beside me, quivering with suppressed merriment, and every second I apprehended some irreverent outburst from her. I pinched her arm sharply.

No one, not even Madam, could slide in a word edgewise while Mr. Barnum boasted of his exploits and of the crowned heads he had shaken by the hand. He expatiated: He told us of the triumphs of Jenny Lind, the Swedish Nightingale, and of General Tom Thumb and his dainty little wife, Lavinia, and how he had bamboozled with his mermaid, and how he had emptied his crowded museum on a busy day to make room for more patrons by exhibiting a flaring sign over a door which read, "This Way to the Egress!" He was a mountebank, but on a majestic scale, and he awed while he amused.

We drew up with a flourish near the ticket booth on Stubby Newell's farm and paid our four dollars for admission. Though it was not yet noon, there was a considerable patronage, and I could see Mr. Barnum counting and calculating. We entered the tent and stood gazing down at the huge stone effigy. Mr. Barnum snorted. His eyes were bright and shrewd. He gazed his fill, and then, walking in his pompous manner, approached Stubby Newell.

"Sir," the great showman said, "my name is Barnum."

"Calc'late I recognized ye from pictures I've seen," Stubby said.

"Are you," asked Mr. Barnum, "the owner of this monstrosity, sir?"

"Ye might say so," admitted Stubby.

"This is an unhandy spot to reach."

"But folks come," Stubby said cannily.

"So it seems. So they do. How many have viewed this object?"

"A goodly number," Stubby said.

"Hey, Stubby!" interrupted a nasal voice, and I turned to see the horsy getup of the country banker, David Hannum.

"What's wanted, Dave?"

"Don't make no dicker with Phineas T. Barnum," David said crisply, "till you've discussed with me. Wouldn't be wise, seems as though. This thing's wuth more'n a shillin' if it fetched Mr. Barnum here from N'Yawk."

"And who," demanded the great man, "are you?"

"Name of Hannum," said Dave. "Hoss trader."

"Mr. Hannum," Barnum said, recognizing a kindred soul, "I did not come here without preliminary investigation. I can tell you, sir, almost to a penny, the receipts of the exhibition. I am able also to inform you that only a small part of the proceeds remains in the hands of Mr. Newell, here. The lion's share is dispatched almost as soon as taken in to one George Hull, cigar manufacturer, of Binghamton. Should I, perhaps, treat with Mr. Hull as the true owner of this—er—phenomenon of the ages?"

He turned on his heel testily and led us back to the carriage, where, with lavish manners, he handed Madam and Lossie into the carriage.

"This trip," he said presently, "has been in vain."

"How, sir," I asked, "would you know that?"

"Young man," Mr. Barnum said, puffing out his cheeks and tossing his head majestically, "there's no man in these United States of America better equipped to recognize scalawags on sight than myself." His face softened into a sly grin. "And why, sir? Because no man in these

United States has invented and carried to success more profitable skulduggeries than myself."

To watch them, you would have thought that Madam Janeway and Lossie were lifetime intimates and closest of friends. You could see, without half trying, that affection had sprung up between them. You could tell it by little side glances and half smiles and touches of the hands. It was dignified on the part of Madam, but prettily eager on the part of Lossie. I had not thought Lossie capable of it, but there was no doubt she was far gone in heroine worship.

Madam purveyed for us a charming luncheon served by her ill-favored butler. At the end of it, she turned to Lossie. "I wonder, honey, if you could entertain Mr. Barnum for five minutes whilst I consult briefly with my legal adviser." It was "honey" now.

She led me into a cozy room off the back parlor which was fitted up as a sort of office, but with feminine ameliorations. She motioned to a comfortable patent rocker, in which I seated myself while she threw back a drapery and disclosed an iron safe which opened with a great key. She exerted some effort to throw wide the heavy door, and I could see within numerous packets of papers and several bundles wrapped in strong paper and further secured by narrow tapes and dabs of red sealing wax. She selected one of these and came to sit at her desk.

"Mr. Applegate," she said, "this, of course, is confidential."

"Between client and lawyer," I said gravely.

"I wish this rather valuable package delivered to Mr.

Watts at his bank. I wish him to deposit it in his vault where it may become instantly available. For sufficient reasons I do not wish to deposit it myself."

"Yes, Madam," said I.

"It contains securities—negotiable securities—to a considerable amount."

"Yes, Madam."

"Which are listed on the wrapping, so there can be no doubt of the contents."

"I understand," said I, as she pushed the packet across to me. I lifted it and examined it. There was indeed a list, but the list was in the form of a communication in spidery handwriting. First I was awed by the value of the contents—upward of two hundred thousand dollars. The writing began: "Dear little Cissie," and continued, though there had been an effort to erase, "This is a tenth part of what I have set aside for you." At some of this I had to guess because the words were illegible because of attempts at erasure. Then followed the list of securities within. At the end was a signature of which only a portion, and that very faint, remained. It consisted of the letters: "D. . . el Dr. w."

Two hundred thousand in the safest of securities— and it but a tenth part of the fortune that had been set aside for Madam Janeway by a man who called her "dear little Cissie." And whose mutilated and erased signature might, if made complete, spell out the name of Daniel Drew. And Daniel Drew's name had appeared without obliteration or erasure on the flyleaf of the Bible that had been upon the table in Banker Watts' parlor. Here was a mystery. How did the good book get on Watts' table? And why?

It was none of my business, even as Madam's lawyer. But in that position I felt my importance. To be attorney for a lady worth two million dollars was something pretty substantial.

"But," I expostulated, "this is a huge sum to entrust to me!"

She laughed merrily. "Before all is done," she said, "I'll trust you with much more than that."

And I, young, stupid, fatuous, felt no premonition whatever.

$* \quad * \quad 5 \quad * \quad *$

THE body of the murdered man was retained as
long as possible in the undertaking parlors in hope of an
identification, but there was none. So he was buried hastily, and it was as if he never had been. He became one of
those mysteries to be referred to on occasion, and there
seemed to be an end of the matter.

Stubby Newell, at great expense of labor and some
of money, had his giant transported to Syracuse, where
it would be handier for the increasing crowds to reach,
as excursions bearing hundreds of the curious came into
town, eager to pay their dollars and behold this controversial marvel. For it was indeed controversial. Parsons,
educators, skeptics, scientists were belaboring one another. Celebrated men came to see and to make public
their opinions. Robert Ingersoll, the famous agnostic,
stared at the figure, hoping, perhaps, to find in it an answer to the riddle of the universe. Andrew White, president of Cornell College, appeared huffily and denounced
it as a fraud. So it went, and the higher tempers ran
among men of religion and of science, the more the public jostled one another to pay their dollars and feast their

eyes. Rumor had it that Stubby Newell, whose lecture had become longer and more eloquent, had sold a share in the giant to David Hannum and some associates, and that an offer from P. T. Barnum had been refused.

My father, a practical man, was among the scoffers, declaring in his abrupt way that Stubby should be arrested for fraud or some other stealthy crime. Lossie's father took the other side of it. Not, I am sure, from conviction, but to amuse himself and to see my father splutter.

But to all of us—at least all of us in our neighborhood—it became a sensation the way Madam Janeway spent her money. After Banker Watts' reception, Madam had received the stamp of approval of our society. She was invited everywhere, and reciprocated with parties and entertainments unrivaled in our history. We were a frugal people who believed that the finest use to which money could be put was to save it. Therefore we were somewhat aghast at the free-handed manner in which Madam tossed dollars about. On Sundays she would put a twenty-dollar bill on the collection plate when our richest church members thought they were being generous with a dollar or with fifty cents. On the slightest excuse she gave expensive presents—and never in a condescending way. She did flamboyant things, but never in a flamboyant manner. Somehow her charm and naturalness made anything she did seem as if it flowed from a simple, generous heart.

She bought a piano for the Sunday-school room. She was forever commissioning me to attend to small matters such as buying Old Man Mullis a pair of crutches or paying the doctor for delivering Mrs. Mertz's eighth baby. She gave a huge dance and imported a fine orchestra from New York to play for it; and she never went on a trip to Boston or New York without taking along with her two or three younger women and treating them most royally. Such spending was outside our experience, but it did not decrease Madam's popularity, nor did it put a stop to speculations as to the amount of her wealth or where all the money came from.

Of course, by now, everybody in town knew that there was some close relationship between her and multimillionaire Dan'l Drew, and it was but natural to conclude that he was the source of her riches. But she never mentioned his name or referred to him in any manner whatever.

The bewildering thing to me was Lossie's infatuation for the older woman. They were inseparable. Lossie became in effect an inmate of Madam's home. They drove together; they shopped together; they promenaded together. Their relationship resembled a schoolgirl crush, except that it seemed to have a firmer and more adult foundation. When I twitted Lossie about it, she only became inscrutable and flouted me. But one thing I noted with interest and some satisfaction, and that was that Miss Lossie never accepted anything of value from Madam, whether it was a piece of jewelry or a trip to New York with expenses paid.

Representing Madam Janeway, as I was supposed to do, consisted more in acting as her escort than in rendering legal services. One afternoon when Madam was newly returned from some journey, she required me to accompany her and Lossie on a drive. It was a beautiful chilly afternoon, with the foliage of our trees making the countryside a flaming wonder of color. Madam fumbled in her reticule and brought out a little leather case and snapped it open. In the satin of it was a jeweled brooch which looked highly expensive to me.

Madam tapped Lossie's hand affectionately. "I got to thinking of you one day," Madam said, "and I missed you. And it seemed I simply had to do something about you. So I went in and bought this trinket for you. Somehow it made me less lonely for you, my dear."

Lossie took the case in her slender fingers and looked at it and admired its contents, and then her pert face became grave. "It's lovely, Madam Cissie," she said, "and it was sweet and generous of you to think of me." Her voice became firmer. "But, Madam, there must be an understanding between us." She nodded her head determinedly.

"What understanding, honey child?"

"That never on any occasion whatever shall you give me a gift more expensive than I can afford to give to you."

"But that, Lossie, is so silly. I have so much money and it gives me such pleasure to spend a little of it on you. The cost means nothing. I'd feel ridiculous giving you a book or a box of bonbons."

Lossie interrupted and shook her head stubbornly. "A book I would like; bonbons I would love. But"—she paused and compressed her lips, so that I knew she meant what she said and would not change her mind—"but if you buy me anything costly, I shall have to return it."

For an instant Madam seemed hurt, but then she smiled and patted Lossie's hand. "Such pride!" she exclaimed, and laughed gaily.

"Madam Cissie," Lossie said, still gravely, "there's a difference between pride and self-respect. If I did not feel this way myself, my father and mother would soon correct me."

For a little time Madam made no response, and then she spoke very gently and sincerely. "I wish," she said, "I understood people like you and your parents. If I could, maybe I'd be more like you, and less like myself."

There could be no doubt of Madam Janeway's kindness and generosity, nor of the lavish manner in which she spent money. She never seemed to give a thought to the cost of a thing she wanted or to the expense of any amusement or recreation that promised pleasure. But, contradictorily, there was economy to the running of her household—economy that amounted almost to niggardliness. Her shopping for groceries and vegetables and meats was done exclusively by the butler, Oscar. And if ever there was a stingy, penny-pinching human being, it was he. He haggled and dickered and demanded. He would bicker over the cost of a fifty-cent tack hammer, and the wages he paid the other servants were lower than those paid by anybody else in town. Probably Madam knew nothing about this, being careless of such details, but there was not a merchant or artisan in our city who did not complain he was losing money on Madam's custom. It was so queer as to be laughable. While Oscar was haggling

68

with a farmer over the price of a peck of potatoes, his mistress would be squandering a couple of hundred dollars on some absurd fancy or kindly charity.

She was a brilliant conversationalist—really a prodigious talker. Her mind was facile and brilliant, and there seemed to be no topic upon which she was not informed nor city in the world which she could not describe in fascinating language. But, voluble as she was, she seldom became specific.

"She rambles," my mother said to Lossie's mother. "She darts. A body can't keep up with her. But after you listen to her an hour, you haven't learned a thing you couldn't read in a book."

"She hops, skips and jumps," agreed Mrs. Fox. "And she's like a punkin seed. You put your finger on her to hold her still and she squirts out in any direction."

"Of reticence," mother said, "she seems to have none. She'll talk about anything. But when she's done, she's told you nothing definite."

"She's a flittermouse," said Mrs. Fox indulgently. "But she's a dear, sweet woman."

Mother sometimes could be persistent. Not that she pursued a topic for any purpose, but she would start on something and just go on and on like perpetual motion.

"She's dear and sweet all right," Mother conceded. "But if you were asked, could you tell anybody where she came from? No, ma'am, you couldn't. Or where she was married, or if she has any children? Or why she came to Syracuse?"

Lossie's mother didn't care. She was not of suspicious or inquiring mind and generally accepted things at their face value.

"Oh, what of it?" she asked with a shrug. "Banker Watts must have looked her up. Bankers are such cautious folks! He never would have given that dinner and reception for her if somebody important hadn't vouched for her. Now would he?"

"I suppose not," mother answered a little dubiously. "But I bet, when you come right down to it, that bankers are as gullible as anybody else. They just make believe they are cautious to impress people."

"Banker Watts," said Lossie's mother, "is a pompous old skeeziks, but he's reliable as an eight-day clock."

"I hear," mother said, changing the subject in a way she had when she was tired of the old one, "that Andrew White is in town to look at that Cardiff Giant and tell everybody just what it is."

Andrew White was the new president of Cornell College up at Ithaca and was rated as a pretty smart man who knew almost everything and wouldn't be easy to bamboozle. So we waited to hear what he would have to say about it. And we heard right away in no uncertain terms.

The stone giant had not yet been lugged here to Syracuse when President White made his first inspection. He, in the interests of veracity, had a meeting in our town with the regents of the State University from Albany and with James Hall, who was the most able paleontologist of the day. This august body did not go so far as to agree that the stone effigy was a petrified man of ancient times. But Hall, most qualified of all of them to speak, declared that it did not date back to the Stone Age, but was the most remarkable object brought to light in this country, and was deserving of the attention of archaeologists.

Mr. White was disgusted and he quoted Schiller's line, " 'Against stupidity the very gods themselves contend in vain.' " He declared the figure to be bogus, a hoax, and all those who believed it either to be a petrified human or a work of great antiquity were credulous simpletons.

But this scientific pronouncement by a distinguished educator seemed to convince nobody. The pastor of one of our principal churches declared, for all to hear, that nobody in his senses could deny that here was a fossilized human being and perhaps one of the giants mentioned in Scripture.

The clergy sided almost unanimously with Stubby Newell and his find. Another eminent preacher was quoted as declaring, "This is not a thing contrived by man, but is the face of one who lived on the earth, the very image and child of God."

Reason and science got scant attention. A trained newspaper observer declared in print that "no piece of sculpture ever produced the awe inspired by this blackened form." He added that the figure was not conceived and executed by any human being.

Ours was a happy day in which any argument between science and the church was automatically decided in favor of religion. So Mr. White's skepticism only served further to advertise the giant and to intensify the eagerness of the public to feast their eyes upon it.

The presence of the patent-medicine show in town did not cut into the receipts of Stubby Newell, for the medicine show was free and attracted mostly local people and canawlers, while the audiences for the Cardiff Giant were mostly excursionists. Lossie and I, when time hung heavily, used to stroll down to the field where the troupe had established itself and watch the performance. Almost every time we attended we saw Oscar, Madam Janeway's butler, lurking on the edge of the crowd, making himself inconspicuous, but always watching with a curiously avid expression upon his cadaverous face. To us, it seemed that he tried to make himself invisible— that it was against his will that he came again and again to see the performance.

"As if," Lossie said with puckered brow, "he were an addict and couldn't help himself."

Which, of course, was nonsense, but Lossie has peculiar notions and a different way of looking at things and of expressing herself. Fond as she seemed to be of Madam, and often as she was in Madam's house, she could not get used to Oscar. "He makes chills run up and down my spine," she said, with a shudder. "As if he weren't human. How can Madam Cissie stand him——"

I'm not imaginative, but a practical sort of person, so I surprised myself and Lossie by saying, "Maybe he's one of those undead creatures—what do you call them? Vampires?"

She nodded sharply. "Maybe we better put some

garlic in our doors and windows," she said. "They can't pass that, and they can't cross running water."

Now Lossie isn't a busybody and she doesn't poke and pry into other people's affairs. But she did take to studying Oscar and watching his movements with a sort of childlike curiosity. And so it came about that on an afternoon—I think it was a Thursday—she mixed me up in the matter—as she had been mixing me up in matters ever since she could toddle.

Madam Janeway was away in Binghamton, whither she had gone alone. I came home from the office a bit early to find Lossie waiting for me in the hammock between our two houses. She jumped up at sight of me and was mysterious and excited.

"You come along with me, Orrin," she commanded.

I held back. "What trouble are you trying to get me into now?" I demanded.

"All right," she said, "then I'll go by myself."

She knew that would fetch me. Sullenly, I followed her. She led me to the corner and then to the street behind Madam's house. We cut through a grove there to where Madam's barn stood at the rear of her lot. She pressed her finger to her lips, cautioning silence. I listened. Someone was inside. I heard a thud, and then, after seconds, another thud.

"What?" I asked.

"Lift me up," she commanded, and I took her under the arms and hoisted her so that she could look through a small, square window. The thuds continued, spaced by ten-second intervals.

"What's that noise?" I asked impatiently, and was rewarded by a kick from her heels. So I dropped her and hoisted myself up and looked inside. In a moment my eyes accustomed themselves to the change in light and I saw Oscar standing in his shirtsleeves next to a table. And on the table were a dozen large and heavy knives. At intervals he would select one, poise it and hurl it with might and main at something. The something was a broad board or pair of boards fastened together to make a surface some four feet wide by six feet high. And on this surface was outlined a female figure in what I took to be tights. It was at this figure that Oscar threw his knives, one after the other, so that the woman was outlined with quivering blades. He never missed. Each knife, as thrown, struck point foremost on the very line outlining the figure. Never had I seen such an exhibition of skill or so sinister an exhibition of steadiness of hand.

I lowered myself and faced Lossie. "How did you know?" I asked.

"I didn't. I only suspected he was up to something. Because every afternoon he comes out here and stays alone in the barn. Butlers don't behave so."

"And, of course, you had to stick in your nose?" I said testily.

"Why, of course," she said, with surprise that I should ask such a question.

"But what does it mean?"

"It means," she said, "that the—the old vampire is better at other things than being a butler."

We were a little surprised that Madam Janeway refused to go with us to see the medicine show, which continued its stay in Syracuse, because she was always so eager for entertainment and amusement. However, as I said to Lossie, everybody is entitled to a couple of inconsistencies. To which Lossie replied that I would be a great deal more interesting if I would develop a couple myself.

And there was another oddity. Madam would have nothing to do with the canal. It was almost as if she resented it and had some private reason for avoiding even conversation about the great, historic, man-made waterway. She had never a kind word to say for canawlers, but always referred to them with contempt. Which was unlike her, for she was a tolerant woman with a soft spot in her heart for all human beings—especially the lowly or unfortunate.

Canawlers were a part of our everyday life, always with us, living their own peculiar, nomadic lives. They were a tribe unto themselves, with a different set of morals and manners. They had their own fierce pride and regarded any person who was not a canawler as inferior and to be suspected.

When Lossie and I were children we never were admonished to have no dealings with canawlers or to stay away from the ditch and the boats that traversed it. We were not forbidden because it never occurred to our fathers and mothers that a pair of well-brought-up children of our social class ever would so far forget themselves as to go near such people. I would never have done so, but Lossie was a cat of another color. Lossie was an obedient little girl and would very seldom disobey a direct command. But she had her own ideas regarding that area of behavior about which there was no direct order. She expressed her conviction when she was very little, and in her succinct manner. "If," she would say, "they don't tell us not to, then we can."

So, being as curious as a kitten, she led me to places where I would not have gone by myself, and one of these places was the basin where canal boats tied up for the night, and where canawlers and their women sat on deck of evenings and drank hard liquor or sang to banjos or engaged in savage fist fights on the towpath.

Now, canawlers are a rough and turbulent set of slatternly women and tobacco-chawing, bewhiskered men. But this I will say for them: children were as safe down there by the basin as they would have been in church. Though they might have heard some unchurchly language—in which the canawlers saw no evil and used as normal means of communication.

Maybe unusual good fortune was ours on our first adventure among these folk. Moored to the spikes was an eighty-foot canal boat embellished by a wide red stripe around its belly. Its name was Lizzie Ann, and lounging near its stern were two people—an enormous, broad-shouldered man with a spreading, golden beard, and a tiny, neat figure of a woman in calico, with cameo-like features and the reddest hair I ever have seen.

Lossie plucked at my arm and we stood staring—

not with thumbs in our mouths as backwoods or Indian children do when staring at something strange. We were too well taught for that.

"Ask," prodded Lossie, "if we can come onto their boat and look at it."

I had no desire to go onto their boat, but the decision was taken away from me. The little woman removed the pipe from her mouth and squinted at us and said, in as soft and musical a voice as ever came to my ears, "Good day to you, moppet."

"Good day, ma'am," Lossie said politely, and I snatched off my cap.

"Hello, bub," said the enormous man to me, and I answered, "How do you find yourself, sir?"

"P'lite," said the big man to the little woman.

"As all git out," said the woman. . . . "You like ginger cookies, you two?"

"Very much indeed," Lossie answered.

"Then come aboard," the woman said. . . . "Zacharias, you fetch up a plate of them gingers and couple glasses of milk. . . . What's your name, moppet?"

"Lossie Fox."

"And yourn, bub?"

"Orrin Applegate."

"Dew tell! We've carried salt west fur your paw."

The yellow-haired giant returned with a plate piled high with ginger cookies and two mugs of milk.

"Mine was named Lizzie Ann," the woman said. "She took sick 'n' died."

"Boat's named fur her," Zacharias explained.

"I calc'late," said the woman to Lossie, "I'll call ye Lizzie Ann. It kind of comforts me to purtend fur a spell."

"That will be nice," Lossie said through a mouthful of cooky. "And what may we call you, ma'am?"

"I'd be gratified if you'd call me maw," the woman said. "But the name they call me by length and breadth of the canawl is Zach Wheelright's woman."

"They're the nicest ginger cookies I ever ate," Lossie said. "Do you keep your horses down there?" she asked, pointing to the deck.

"Comfortable as bugs in a rug," said Zacharias. "Driver's gone uptown to git drunk."

Somehow, this information did not shock us. It seemed in keeping with the surroundings.

"It must," Lossie said, "be lovely riding all day long, day after day, on a nice boat like this, Mrs. Wheelright."

"Hain't Mrs. Wheelright," said the woman placidly. "Jest Zach's woman. Been so fifteen year. Naw, Zach 'n' me never got to stand up 'fore a parson. Zach wouldn't have it, and Zach's a man firm set in his ways. My paw he told Zach he couldn't have me 'less he married me. Wa-al, Zach he didn't have no objections, but he wouldn't allow nobuddy to tell him what to do."

"So what did you do?" Lossie asked.

"Why, Zach he turned to me and says loud fur all to hear, 'Susie, I claim you're my wife.' So, seein' how things were, I answers right back, 'And I claim ye fur my husband.' "

"An', by dang," Zach said, shading his oath in deference to Lossie's ears, "I'll claw the gizzard out of any that lets on there's a firmer way of gittin' wedded."

Well, we stayed there as long as we dared, and then we had to go home, so Lossie said, "Good-by for now, maw." And Zach Wheelright's woman answered, "Good-by, Lizzie Ann." But she didn't offer to touch Lossie; only sort of stretched out a hand toward her. And Mr. Wheelright, he grinned broadly at us and said, "Come visit us any time we tie up. Keep an eye out fur us. It pleasures maw to have a moppet aboard."

We went home, but it did not seem advisable to tell our parents about where we had been or what we had talked about. But after that we kept an eye out for the Lizzie Ann, and we never failed to go aboard when she tied up in the basin. And gradually we got acquainted with a great many other canawlers, who were not offish with us, because we were such good friends of Zach Wheelright and his woman.

We heard, I'm afraid, much talk that was not fit for Lossie's ears—or for mine, for that matter. But it didn't seem to do any harm and it didn't seem wicked to us because, probably, it wasn't spoken with wicked intent by the canawlers, but was just the way they talked. And it got so that they thought a heap of Lossie and she could make them do things nobody else could. Like when she saw Sam'l Dwiggs and Noah Clem trying to tear out each other's gullets on the path, and everybody was keeping his distance because they were crazy mad. But Lossie walked right up to them and almost in between them, and said real sharp, "You stop that this minute or I'll take you both in hand." And the miracle was they stopped and big Noah hoisted Lossie in his great hands and bellowed out, "This here moppet's the bully of the canal, 'n' I'll gut any man says to the contrary!" And, still holding Lossie aloft, he leaped high into the air and cracked his heels together and let out a panther whoop that would have scared a body most to death.

But Lossie wasn't frightened, and she sort of tugged at Noah's matted whiskers, and said, but not sharp, "Put me down, great ox, before you wrinkle my dress."

This was all years ago, but, unbeknownst to our folks and the people among whom we lived, we continued to visit the basin and the Lizzie Ann, and, if the truth were told, certain other less reputable canal boats.

* * 6 * *

I WENT out to get my lunch and strolled down toward the basin and there, just pulling in, was the Lizzie Ann. I watched them make fast and unhitch the horses from the tow rope and drive them aboard and down to their stable, and then, not waiting even for a cup of coffee, I hurried home and around to the side of Lossie's house and whistled our urgent whistle. She stuck her head out of her bedroom window, and I beckoned and said, "They're tied up in the basin."

"Be right down," she said, and was as good as her word. So we hurried down and along the towpath to the basin and jumped aboard the Lizzie Ann. Zach and his woman were just sitting down to eat, and the driver was there. When they saw us, Zach let out a great whoop, and in a twinkling there were two more places and we were eating as finely cooked a meal as ever passed my lips. Not served, of course, with proper decorum, but fit for a king. And Lossie called Zack's woman "maw" and Zach's woman called her "Lizzie Ann," and Zach grinned and belched, and the driver said nary a word, as was his custom.

81

"If you're going to be in till morning," Lossie said, "you ought to go up and see the medicine show. It's free."

"Medicine show!" Zach said ruminatively. "The's medicine shows 'n' medicine shows. This one got a tooth puller?"

"Quickest you ever saw," Lossie said.

"And maybe a mesmerizer?"

"There's a mesmerizer," I said.

"And maybe——" Zach said more slowly, looking at me under his bushy brows in a shrewd, sly manner. "And maybe a gent that stands off and throws knives at his woman, and her standin' against a board. Never slices her even once."

"No, Mr. Wheelright," Lossie said, "there's no knife thrower."

"Be ye certain sure?"

"Positive," Lossie said.

"If they was sich a one," Zach said ponderously, "I'd advise ye emphatic to stay away from there like the' was smallpox."

"That's right, Lizzie Ann," said Zach's woman. "Him that Zach refers to has got rattlesnake pizen in his veins instid of blood. My man don't back off from nobody along the canawl from Troy to Buffalo, includin' the feeders, but he gives ground to that livin' skeleton, and don't take no shame fur it."

"About six feet and three inches high?" asked Lossie.

"All of that."

"Wide shoulders and skinny arms and legs and a head like a death's head?"

"That's the spittin' image of him," Zach said. "And the funny thing! His woman that he throwed knives at was sweet 'n' perty as a princess in one of them fairy stories."

"Like I used to tell Lizzie Ann," said Zach's woman. . . . "Didn't I, Lizzie Ann?"

And Lossie replied without hesitation, "And you told them so well, maw."

The little woman's eyes softened and brimmed, and she smiled a wonderful smile at Lossie.

"We both know 'tain't so, don't we?" Zach's woman asked.

"Of course," Lossie agreed.

"But it don't do no harm," the little woman said pleadingly. "And—and it pleasures me a heap sight."

"To be sure, maw," Lossie said. "We'll keep right on."

"All the same," Zach said with a nod of his great, golden head, "I hain't agoin' to traipse to no medicine show. It'd leave a sour taste in my mouth."

"We want no truck with sich," his woman agreed.

Lossie and I stayed the afternoon, and there were callers and talk, some of it loud and some of it savage, about killings and gouging out of eyes, and about the abominable habits of lock tenders, and about high waters and births with no attending physician, and about how the railroads were ruining business on the canal. Late in the afternoon, Lossie and I shook hands all around and went home to supper, because there would have had to be explanations if we absented ourselves. And Lossie never was one for explanations.

"You start explaining something," she was wont to say, "and sure's shooting you get tripped up into the soup. Just keep quiet and act natural and questions don't get asked."

"Do you suppose," I asked, "that Mr. Wheelright's knife thrower and Madam Janeway's Oscar are one and the same?"

"Well, now, Orrin," she said, and became patronizing, as she did when she wanted to irritate me, "I should just hazard a guess that, as Madam's attorney at law and counselor in chancery, you would stay away from wanting the answer to that question."

Though Lossie is younger than I, and a girl to boot, I have sometimes an uncomfortable feeling that she is far shrewder than I. In this instance it was so. I was sure she was right and that the last piece of information I wanted to possess was Oscar's identification as Zach's knife thrower and Zach's woman's monster with rattlesnake venom in his veins instead of blood.

Twenty-four guests could be seated around Madam Janeway's dining table, and Lossie and I were included in the number. It was a formal affair. Invitations had been handsomely engraved. The affair was to be in honor of Horatio Dewitt, president of one of Albany's largest banks. Another out-of-town guest was Jethro Willis, banker, of Binghamton. Of course, Mr. and Mrs. Watts

were there. Never had I seen a table so beautifully fur-
bished with damask and silver and rare china. Lossie was
very grand and dignified and beautiful, with her chin
high and her cheeks flushed with excitement. It was not
easy to imagine that she could be more at home in the
cabin of a canal barge with canawlers for companions
than she was in this society.

Little parcels were at each place—favors, I believe
they were called—a gift for every guest. Which, I understand, is a newfangled custom aping European manners. I opened my packet and found a pair of gold cuff
buttons set with some sort of stone which I did not recognize. Little exclamations were audible as guest after
guest disclosed the contents of his packet. If my gift was
a fair example, then the favors must have cost Madam
Janeway better than five hundred dollars.

"Why, Madam," I heard the Albany banker exclaim,
"Mr. Vanderbilt himself could not be more lavish."

She gave him her smile. "Trifles," she said with a
shrug.

In serving the dinner, Oscar was assisted by a flock
of waiters imported for the purpose—trained and deft
men. And the food! Lucullus could not have purveyed
rarer dishes—oysters from Maryland, and terrapin and
guinea hen and ices and a variety of wines. I watched
Lossie sharply to be sure I managed each dish with proper
decorum and did not use the wrong silver utensil.

Between two of the courses I heard Banker Willis
speak to Banker Watts.

"I hear tell," he said, "that they're exhibiting that

stone thingamajig here. The one dug up in Cardiff."

"They are, indeed, Mr. Willis, and taking in money hand over fist." Mr. Watts cleared his throat. "Maybe I shouldn't mention it, but most of the takings go to your town."

"Dew tell!" Willis exclaimed.

"To a man named George Hull—cousin, so I'm told, to the one who dug up the giant."

"George Hull, hey? A scalawag as ever was. No respect for man or God. Not George. Pokes fun at everything."

"Including, I'll bet," Lossie whispered in my ear, "Mr. Jethro Willis."

"He don't deny being one of them agnostics like Ingersoll," Mr. Willis went on testily. "Lets on he despises folks. Says most people would rather be bamboozled than to see the truth. I heard him say tother day that it was easier to make people give credit to a farfetched lie than it was to a simple fact."

"Well," Banker Watts said shortly, "whatever his beliefs, he makes 'em pay."

"I hear tell," Lossie's father said, "that Barnum tried to buy it."

"So it's rumored," said Mr. Watts.

After the dinner was over, we repaired to the parlor, and there obese little Jethro Willis singled me out. "Orrin Applegate, hain't ye?" he asked.

"That's my name, sir," I answered. He was a crude man without elegance, and I wondered at his presence there.

"Her lawyer, ain't you?" he asked.

"I act for her sometimes."

"Rich woman, from what I hear."

"She seems," I said offishly, "to be in good circumstances."

"What's this about Dan'l Drew?" he asked in an oily whisper.

"I have no knowledge of Mr. Drew, sir."

"And wouldn't let on if you had," he said, nodding his bald head. "Naow listen," he said. "I come over from Binghamton to see if I couldn't pick up a mite of business from her. Be an advantage to her to spread her custom around. Hey?" His little, greedy eyes puckered up at me. "You're her lawyer. You got influence. If you was to swing suthin' my way, I'd see ye didn't lose by it." He twisted his head to look into the small library which Madam used as an office. "Hear she's got a safe in there chuck full of stocks 'n' bonds."

"I cannot," I said grandly, "discuss Madam's affairs with anyone."

"To be sure," he said wheedlingly. "To be sure. But don't forget what I said. You won't lose nothin' by it."

I walked away from him and sought Lossie, but again she was the center of a group of men old enough to know better. She was queening it and had not so much as a glance for me. You would have thought she had been brought up to be a grand society lady with all the airs and gestures and coquetry. I wanted to walk up behind her and say, "Hey, there, your pa's just a salt boiler like mine. Come down off your high horse." But I didn't.

I went over and leaned against the wall next the archway that gave into Madam's office, and through the portieres I heard talking. I had no intention to eavesdrop. I was down in the mouth and, I expect, sullen. So I just stood there, and in a moment I heard a low-voiced conversation. Madam was there and a man whose voice I did not recognize. I did not mean to pay attention, but words came to my ears spoken in a shrill squeaky voice.

"The little fat fool from Binghamton's swallowed it, hook, line and sinker," he said.

Madam's reply was so softly uttered that I could not distinguish what she said.

"But," went on the skirling voice, "the Albany one is a cat of a different color."

"Shrewd and experienced," Madam said distinctly.

"Treated right," the voice said, "they're the easiest. They think they're so smart nobody'd dare try to put it over 'em. I calc'late," he went on, "we better give him the extry-special treatment."

"Nothing blatant," Madam said sharply.

"Smooth as silk," was the reply, and Oscar, the butler, strode through the archway, not noticing me, and headed for the rear of the house.

It was puzzling. It was not exactly a conversation one would expect to hear between a butler and his mistress, but it meant nothing to me. Madam was different from other people and you expected certain eccentricities from her. I dismissed the matter from my mind.

Perhaps half an hour later the doorbell sounded and I saw Oscar scurrying to answer it. Madam lifted her head as though listening, and then made her way across the room to where Horatio Dewitt was conversing with Lossie's father. She touched him playfully with her fan and said something that made him laugh. Oscar stood in the door looking about until he saw Madam, and then he went to her, a little silver tray in his hand on which rested an envelope.

"Madam," he said woodenly, "the messenger said this was urgent."

She took the envelope in her slender fingers and looked up at Banker Dewitt and shrugged. "You'll pardon me?" she asked.

"Certainly," he said politely.

The envelope was sealed with red wax, but she contrived to tear it open. She uttered a little exclamation, for it contained a stock certificate. From where I stood I could see that it had to do with the Erie Railroad, but her thumb covered the spot where the number of shares it represented was stamped.

"What a nuisance," she said. "But I'd best put it in my safe. Just some Erie bonds I had converted into stock."

"Naturally," Banker Dewitt said respectfully.

She turned lightly and the envelope with its broken seals dropped unnoticed to the floor as she walked away. Lossie's father saw it and stooped to pick it up. You could hear him suck in his breath. And then he was indiscreet, as he so often was.

"Gosh all hemlock!" he exclaimed. "Look at this!"

He held it up in his astonishment, and Dewitt could

see the name and return address. The name was Daniel Drew!

"Get that out of sight!" snarled Banker Dewitt.

"Out of sight," said Lossie's father, who always would have his joke, "but not out of mind."

I felt Jethro Willis' beady eyes fixed avidly on my face. "Mr. Applegate," he said, "you was clost enough to see."

"To see what?" I demanded ungraciously.

"The return address onto that envelope," he said. "It'll be wuth money to me to know."

"Sir," said I righteously, "if you weren't three times my age I'd take you by the collar and throw you out of this house."

He sneered at me. "Uppity, hey? Mebby the day'll come when ye won't be so doggoned segacious with me."

Again I turned away, but I kept my eye on him. He worked his way to the dining room, where Oscar was superintending the clearing up of the room. Jethro walked up to him and spoke. Then, sneakily, he reached into his hip pocket for his wallet and extracted a bill. It was a yellow bill. He handed it to Oscar, who peered about him cautiously and then bent to whisper in Willis' ear. What had happened was apparent. The beady-eyed little banker had bribed Oscar to give him the name of Daniel Drew.

My duty was clear. I sought Madam Janeway and drew her aside."

"Madam Cissie," I said, "something just happened that disturbs me."

"So, very properly, you came to tell me about it," she smiled.

"That letter you just received," said I. "You dropped the envelope."

"How stupid of me," she said. "How horridly stupid."

"Mr. Dewitt," I said, "read the return address."

To this she made no reply.

"That little twerp, Jethro Willis, tried to bribe me to tell him what it was."

She touched my wrist and smiled at me. "I knew," she said, "that I could trust you implicitly."

"But," I said gravely, "I fear you cannot trust your butler."

"Oscar!" she exclaimed.

"Yes," I answered. "For a twenty-dollar bill he gave the information to Willis."

Again she patted my arm. "Don't worry," she said sweetly. "I'll attend to Oscar. Depend upon it, Orrin, he'll tell Mr. Willis nothing that will do him any good. You're a sweet boy." And then, "Lossie looks tired. Why don't you escort her home?"

"Yes, ma'am," I said, "I'll do just that."

Madam Janeway was thoughtful. There was a line between her beautiful eyes. She held up her hand. "But wait a moment," she said. "Lossie can stay a few minutes more. Will you perform a slight service for me?"

"Certainly, Madam," I responded.

"Will you ask Banker Dewitt to step into my office? Bring him, Orrin, and remain yourself." She smiled. "As my confidential representative."

For an instant I remembered that odd conversation between Madam and her peculiar butler in which the name of Mr. Dewitt had come up, and which seemed to hint that he should be convinced of something. But it was only a fleeting thought. Not even a slight suspicion. For I, like everyone else who came in contact with her, was obsessed by Madam's person, and her intelligence and her charm. To say nothing of her obvious wealth.

I sought out Mr. Dewitt and requested him to accompany me to Madam's office which he did readily. She was seated behind her desk, holding in her hands a large manilla envelope which bulged with bulky contents.

"Thank you, Mr. Dewitt, for humoring a whim," she said graciously. "By reputation you are well known to me, both as a banker of ability but also as a man of integrity."

"You are more than kind, Madam," he said.

"Therefore I venture to ask your advice. I do not even ask you to keep the matter confidential, though I know you will be discreet. I have here a communication from The Mercantile Bank of New York. Who represent a—" There came a slight hesitation. "—a valued friend of mine." She held out a communication on the letterhead of the New York bank, first to Mr. Dewitt and then, when he had read it attentively, to me. As I read it my eyes bugged.

"Dear Madam:" it said. "We have been instructed by a certain individual to transmit to you an additional five hundred thousand dollars in the common stocks of the

Erie, The New York Central, and The Western Union Telegraph Company. This completes the amount our client agreed to settle upon you. You are instructed to treat this transaction with your usual discretion."

The letter was signed, *The Mercantile Bank of New York*, by— and the signature was an illegible scrawl— Vice President.

"You are seeking advice in the circumstances, Madam?" asked Mr. Dewitt.

Madam tapped the fat manilla envelope with a tapering finger. "As to whether I should retain these securities, sir, or sell them at the market and invest the proceeds in Government bonds."

It is to be noted that Banker Dewitt did not ask to examine the envelope's contents. Nor would I have done so. Madam inspired confidence.

"By all means, Madam," said Dewitt, "considering the state of the market and—er—the, shall we say source from which they came?—I would recommend that they be retained. You cannot go wrong."

"I'm grateful to you, Mr. Dewitt. You put my mind at rest."

She arose in dismissal, gave him her hand and a smile. Then she turned to me.

"My friend," she said, "now you may take Lossie home."

* * 7 * *

I WAS sitting in my office reading Kent's Commentaries when the door opened without the formality of a knock and two gentlemen entered. I recognized the first as banker David Hannum, character and horse trader, and the second as big George Hull, from Binghamton, where he manufactured cigars.

"'Mornin', Orrin," Mr. Hannum said. "Know George Hull, don't ye?"

I stood up and offered my hand and invited them to be seated. "What service can I render you gentlemen?" I asked.

"Want some papers drawed up," Hannum said. "Figgered you, bein' jest a beginner, 'd do the job cheap."

This was not exactly complimentary, but I made no comment.

"If ye wa'n't perty smart," Hannum said, "that woman wouldn't be hirin' ye."

"It's a kind of a bill of sale we want drawn," Hull said. "Unusual bill of sale for an unusual piece of proppity. I'm sellin' two thirds of the Cardiff Giant."

"You are selling?" I exclaimed. "I thought Stubby

94

Newell owned it!"

"Ye don't need to fret about that," Hannum said. "George has got a title to it that contents me."

"Very well, Mr. Hannum. And what are the terms of the sale?"

"I'm payin', on behalf of me and others, thirty-seven thousand dollars fur a two-thirds interest in the critter. George here agrees we shall take over management 'n' handle all business matters. Accounts to be rendered every three months." He had not taken off his horseman's cap. Now he pushed it to one side and scratched his head. "Kind of got the best of P. T. Barnum," he said, with a shrewd, self-satisfied grin. "He wanted it fur that New York museum of hisn."

"I venture to say ye haven't heard the last of him," Hull remarked dryly. "Next to Bob Ingersoll, he's the man I admire most. Got rich bamboozlin' suckers."

"Use the right bait at the right time," Hannum said through his nose, "and everybuddy's a sucker."

"The bigger the swindle," Hull said, "the more folks'll b'lieve it."

"Do you mean," I asked undiplomatically, "that the Cardiff Giant is a swindle?"

"Some says yes," Hull replied. "Some says no. Me, I got no opinion. The stronger they argyfy the more dollars roll in."

"Git to whizzin', Orrin," Hannum said impatiently. "We hain't got all night."

I took foolscap paper and a new pen from a drawer and wrote rapidly. I wanted to impress these men with my ability, so I wrote without hesitation. But that was a mistake. When I had completed two copies for their signatures and they had signed and Hannum had given Hull his check for the purchase price, Hannum coughed dryly. "Haow much do I owe ye, Orrin?"

"Five dollars," I said boldly.

"Five dollars!" Hannum exclaimed. "Fur a job ye done like greased lightnin'? Give ye two-fifty."

"You," I said with such determination as I could muster, "are not paying me for writing a few words. What you're paying me for is knowing what words to use. My price is five dollars."

Hannum scowled at me an instant; then he slapped his thigh and bellowed with laughter. "Bub," he said, "that's the way to talk up! By dad! Make up your mind what you're wuth 'n' never let nobuddy beat ye daown. You'll be gittin' more business of mine."

They walked out of my office and I pocketed the five-dollar bill with elation. It was a splendid fee. If the time ever came when I could take in that much every day I would really be established. It would amount to fifteen hundred dollars a year.

I returned to Kent's Commentaries and read until noon, when I put on my hat and walked home to lunch. I saw Madam Janeway's equipage stop under her porte-cochere and Madam and Lossie alight and go into the house. I ate a leisurely dinner with mother and father. In those days the heavy meal of the day was served at noon. I walked back to the office through air that was becoming brisk, hinting of a winter not too many weeks away. I sat at my desk, putting away from me an urge to lift my feet to its top and be comfortable. If I permitted a laxity such as that when I was alone, it might grow upon me until I would exhibit an undignified behavior in public. It was fortunate that I maintained an erect posture, because there came a knock on my door. Upon my invitation, a man entered whom I did not at first recognize. He was tall, erect and fashionably dressed.

"Mr. Applegate?" he said.

"How do you do, sir?" I inquired.

"My name is Gideon Weeks," he said. "I have seen you frequently in our audiences, accompanied by a charming young lady."

I recognized him then, of course. He seemed to be the manager or proprietor of the medicine show, as well as one of its entertainers. It was he who did the actual selling of the bottles of medicine while he performed quite startling feats of legerdemain. He was an unusually handsome man with burnside whiskers and a humorous, ready smile. Lossie had thought, on that day when we had seen the troupe debark from the packet boat, that she had seen him before in other circumstances, and now that I scrutinized him close at hand I felt that I, too, had encountered him somewhere in the past. It was an elusive impression.

"You came," he said, "to see our performance so often that I inquired who you were." His charming smile flashed. "And so, when I had need of a lawyer, I naturally came to you."

That did not follow naturally, but I saw no reason to argue the point.

"And how may I serve you, Mr. Weeks?"

"I understand," he said, "that lawyers sometimes accept cases and agree to speculate on the outcome. I mean they agree to take as their fee a share of the sum awarded as damages."

"A contingent fee," I said. "It is done."

"Would you accept a case on that basis, Mr. Applegate?"

"That," I told him, "would depend upon the nature of the case and the probability of winning a verdict."

"Of course," he agreed. "It is a case of personal injury. A small boy—you have seen him; he is our mesmeric subject—was struck down by one of Whitman's drays, driven at reckless speed by a drunken driver."

"Do you," I inquired, "stand *in loco parentis* to this boy?"

"No," he replied. "He is a homeless orphan that Signor Manetti befriended." Signor Manetti was their mesmerist.

"Before he would be permitted to figure in a lawsuit," I explained, "it would be necessary for the court to appoint a guardian *ad litem*."

He nodded his understanding and proceeded to recite to me the details of the accident and the names of witnesses who would be willing to testify to what they had seen. Upon his relation, it seemed to be a perfect example of negligence, if not worse. Of course, I would have to examine these witnesses and form an opinion as to their credibility.

"How seriously is the child injured?" I asked.

"Dislocations, bruises, contusions, and something seems to be amiss with his spine."

"Very well," I told him. "If my investigations bear out your story, I will accept the case on a contingent basis—fifty per cent of the damages awarded. In view of the fact that I take all the risks, it is not exorbitant."

"Very well," he agreed. "Business has not been too flourishing or I would retain you on a regular basis. We have had desertions, Mr. Applegate. Our show is not the colossal thing it once was. Our strong man took other employment, and our Venetian glass blowers disappeared. Our four jubilee singers left us. We have been unable to replace them."

"Is that the complete list of deserters?" I asked. To this day I do not know why.

"It is not," he said. "We had a marvelous knife thrower and his lady, at whom he threw his knives, and who doubled as a singer of ballads."

"Indeed!" I exclaimed. "Indeed!"

Even as I made this exclamation an alarm bell rang in my head, not loudly and urgently, but faintly and almost inaudibly. I did not heed it. On the surface there was nothing to put me on my guard, and the possibility —probability—of a fee amounting to a couple of thousand dollars blunted my caution.

I wrote down the names of witnesses and their addresses.

"These," I told him, "I will interview and give you

my decision tomorrow afternoon, if you will call again."

He arose, and his height was imposing. I took his extended hand and he left the office. I was pleased with myself. In one day an actual cash fee of five dollars and a damage case which very well might earn me five hundred times that much. I wanted to go home and boast a little to father and mother—but mainly to Lossie Fox. For some reason I found it essential to impress her with my importance.

I sat thinking about my latest client and of my impression that I had seen him somewhere before. Then I became certain that I never had seen him before in some other environment. It was not that. I became convinced that it was a resemblance, a similarity to someone I did know. Mr. Gideon Weeks bore a remarkable resemblance to someone with whose face I was familiar. But struggle as I might, I could not identify that other face.

I closed the office early because I wanted, I suppose, to strut a little. I should have known Lossie better than to try it on her. She always had had a very special way of pricking bubbles, especially if I had blown them. I walked rapidly home through autumn air that was agreeably weighted with the odor of burning leaves. Lossie, a long-handled wooden rake in her hands, was scuffling through the maple leaves which had fallen thickly on our lawn. She waved at me and called to me to get a rake.

"Bonfire!" she cried out, almost as excitedly as she would have done ten years before. "The leaves are dry as dry!"

"Why," I asked patronizingly, "don't you grow up?"

She leaned on her rake, very young and lovely and somehow elfin, and made a face at me and said, "Young spriggins, when I grow up I'll grow up. I won't just puff up." She waggled her thumb at the barn and commanded, "Go get a rake." There was no slight resemblance now between this *gamine* and the grand lady she had learned how to become when she saw reason for it. I started back for the barn obediently, and she called after me, "When you come back, I'll listen to your brags!"

I felt my ears reddening, and almost went into the house in a huff, but that would only have drawn more tormenting remarks from Miss Lossie; so I came back with a rake and commenced to help her pile up leaves in the driveway, where we could set them ablaze.

"All right, Alexander," she said presently, "what worlds did you conquer today?"

"I thought," I said, and the hurt of it must have been audible in my voice, "that you might have been glad to hear about it."

Instantly she was contrite. "Of course I want to hear about it, Orrin," she said in a gentler tone. "But you exasperate me. You're so biggety."

"I had two clients today," I said.

"Oh, how nice!" she exclaimed genuinely. "Can you tell me?"

"One of them," I said, "was David Hannum. He came in with George Hull. To get me to draw a bill of sale of the Cardiff Giant. I charged him five dollars," I said smugly.

"So now," she responded, "you can buy me an enormous box of candy."

"The other client," I went on, "was Gideon Weeks, the medicine-show man."

She dropped her rake and grasped my arm. "That handsome young man!" she exclaimed and gave my arm a little shake, saying urgently, "What did he want, Orrin? What did he want?"

"That little boy that they mesmerize," I said. "He was run over by a dray. I'm to sue for damages. I took it," I said, "on a contingent basis, and my fee might be as much as two thousand dollars." I paused to let her exclaim, but she did not exclaim. She became very grave.

"I don't like you to have that man for a client," she said.

"Why in the world not?" I demanded. And then I remembered the first time we had seen the medicine-show troupe and Mr. Weeks, and how Lossie had said she had seen him sometime, somewhere, and had seemed disturbed about it. "Do you know, it's a funny thing," I said before she could answer, "but today I had the same impression you had—that I had seen him before. But when I got to thinking it over, I knew I never had seen him before, but someone who looked like him."

"Who was it?" she asked.

"I don't know. I can't figure it out."

Just then Madam Janeway's splendid team of horses

drew her carriage down the street and turned in at her drive. She waved to us gaily.

"It's odd," I said thoughtfully, for my mind was still upon Weeks and his troupe of performers, "that Madam never will go with us to see the show. She always wants to be at everything that goes on."

"Nothing," Lossie said solemnly, "is strange when you understand the reason for it."

"Do you?" I asked.

She was very pensive. Her enthusiasm for raking leaves and building a bonfire seemed to have abated. Her lovely eyes were dark and brooding.

"I hope I don't know the reason," she said, "and I hope I never find out."

"I see by the paper," said Lossie's father in his dry, ironic voice, "that they're havin' quite a time of it down to New York. Mobs looting grocery stores and the like of that."

"Distress is said to be acute," replied Madam Janeway, who was the dinner guest of the Foxes at a casual evening gathering.

"But Syracuse," went on Uncle Lander, "is resting on a firmer financial foundation. Paper says our drugstores sold fifteen thousand bottles of bitters and three thousand two-ounce bottles of soothin' syrup this year. Yes'm, to the virtuous and nondrinking citizens of this town. Calc'late our future's safe, though I'd admire to know which sect prefers soothing syrup to bitters."

"Lander Fox!" his wife said sharply.

"Panic-proof business," Uncle Lander persisted. "I calc'late to argue Silas here to quit salt boilin' 'n' go into patent medicine. In addition to making money, it's got what you might call its humanitarian aspects. Yup. Think how many old wimmin it solaces for bein' wives to deacons and elders and such like who have no other high jinks this side of the grave."

"Madam Janeway," said embarrassed Mrs. Fox, "I hope you'll pay no attention to my husband. . . . Lander Fox, you're irreverent."

"Jest observing," said Uncle Lander. "Like every time I've dropped around to this Umatilla Indian medicine show, Deacon Milliken's coachman's been there buyin' two bottles. Looks like somebody's layin' in a bulwark against the coming of a drought." He uttered an arid cackle. "Besides which, this Umatilla elixir has taken pains not to disguise the taste of pure whisky."

"The poor, starved things!" Madam Janeway said sympathetically.

Uncle Lander was on his way and not to be stopped. "I'm not a drinking man, as all Syracuse can testify," he said, "but I've tried 'em all, in the interests of science— Kickapoo Elixir of Life, Hoffenderfer's Bitters 'n' a dozen others—and I'm in a position to testify this Umatilla tipple is the tastiest of all. Also," Uncle Lander finished up, "they got the best show. . . . You seen it, Madam?"

"I've not seen it," Madam said not unpleasantly. "That sort of exhibition wouldn't entertain me, I fear.

I have avoided it."

Lossie whispered in my ear almost inaudibly, "And it hasn't seen her."

"What do you mean by that?" I demanded.

"Since they've been in town," Lossie said, "Madam has been practically invisible."

"Nonsense," I said tartly.

"What did you say, Orrin?" my mother asked.

"Nothing, mother. I was just telling Lossie she was talking nonsense."

"As she so often does," said her father, with a grin of affection in her direction. "But look out, Orrin. Sometimes her nonsense has more bite to it than other folks' logic."

On occasion I became seriously impatient with Lossie, for she blurted. She would up and out with things for no apparent reason at all, and they could be embarrassing.

"The Umatilla tribe," she said distinctly, "have become clients of Orrin's."

Madam looked from Lossie to me with arched brows. One could see that she was not pleased.

"Is this true, Orrin?" she asked.

"Not exactly," I told her. "Not definitely. I've been asked by their Mr. Weeks to take a personal-injury case on a contingent basis."

"But you have not bound yourself?"

"Not, Madam, until I have investigated the evidence carefully."

"Madam Cissie," Lossie said with vast sobriety,

"Orrin always can be relied upon to look before he leaps. There's no fun reading a story when you always know what's going to happen in the next chapter." Her temper suddenly was up, as happened sometimes so unaccountably. She seemed to have forgotten that she and I were not alone. "Orrin Applegate," she said sharply, "do you have to be a model young man? If just once in your life you'd do something unexpected, like—like getting in a fight or cutting up a caper!"

"One flibbertigibbet in a neighborhood is enough," I retorted.

Madam seemed to be distrait. What had started out as a merry evening began to drag. For a time, conversation languished. Even Lossie withdrew into herself, and Uncle Lander's store of funny reminiscences dried up. So it was that shortly after nine Madam Janeway, politely concealing a yawn, announced that she had spent a tiring day and longed for her bed. She smiled at me.

"I wonder, Orrin," she said, "if you would escort me across the street." She glanced around the company half humorously. "A small matter of business upon which I wish to consult my attorney."

After we had crossed the street and mounted Madam's porch, the door was opened to us by the butler, Oscar. The sight of the man always upset me. He was a strange-looking creature, and I marveled that so dainty a person as Madam could tolerate him about her. I wondered if she knew how truly weird a servant she harbored, with his knife throwing out in her barn.

She led me into her little office and dismissed Oscar. "That will be all," she said to him. "You may go to bed, Oscar."

He stood still and expressionless, his pale eyes unwinking before he turned on his heel and withdrew. Perhaps I made some movement, perhaps I even shuddered. At any rate, Madam became aware of my aversion for the man.

"Oscar," she said, "fails to make a happy impression. But he has qualities, Orrin. His has not been a happy life. I do not know what I would do without him."

She bade me be seated and then she leaned forward a little with earnest face.

"Orrin," she said gravely, "you can learn the law from books. You can commit to memory every rule and statute. You can be letter perfect in every printed word, but that does not make you a lawyer."

I waited. This was a strange beginning for a consultation between attorney and client. "No, Orrin," she continued. "It's not enough to know the law; you must know what to do with it. To be a great lawyer you must have experience in the everyday affairs of life. You must know human beings and what arouses their emotions and how they react when their emotions are aroused. Through experience you must learn what to expect in a given set of circumstances."

"Yes, ma'am," I responded, still bewildered.

"You have to know the acts wicked people have perpetrated, and why good people have slipped. The more you know about what has actually happened, and what people really have done, the better lawyer you will be."

"That is undoubtedly true, Madam," I agreed.

"Give time to reading about crimes and plots and chicaneries, and remember the details, so that you will recognize them when you encounter them. Men do not invent new wickednesses; they simply repeat old crimes or adapt old ones to fit their needs. So, Orrin, the more you have studied these matters and read of them and discussed them, the more likely you will be to recognize them in your practice and to thwart them."

"A wide field of study, ma'am," I said.

"But fascinating," she rejoined.

She arose and opened the iron safe. Inside I saw shelves and compartments and pigeonholes crammed with papers and documents and what appeared to be securities. She withdrew a volume of the scrapbook variety and spread it on her desk.

"I," she said, "have made a pastime of clipping from newspapers accounts of clever or unusual crimes. There are hundreds of such clippings here. I find them amusing and sometimes useful."

She turned pages until, apparently, she came to what she sought.

"Please," she said crisply, "state the particulars of this injury case you have been asked to take."

I did so in detail. When I was quite through, she smiled, arched her brows and asked, "Can you describe the man who brought this case to your office?"

I did so with some accuracy, for I remembered him well—and besides, there was that haunting impression that I had seen him elsewhere, or someone resembling him. She nodded emphatically and then read aloud from her scrapbook:

" 'A novel fraud was detected here yesterday by Doctor J. M. Pettigrew. A small boy for whom damages were claimed by reason of personal injuries was examined by this physician after others had pronounced his injuries to be serious and genuine. It was detected that the boy possessed an unusual facility. He could at will dislocate almost any joint in his small body and so appear to have suffered great physical damage. The boy and his accomplices vanished before they could be arrested and brought to justice. The boy was a weakly wizened lad; his principal accomplice was a handsome blond man in his early thirties whose business was the selling of patent medicine.' "

It seemed to me, as one who delights in facts, that here was a very poor account of the affair, even for a country newspaper. Names had not appeared important to the writer, nor other vital particulars. But even so, insufficient as it was, it was sufficiently ample to shock me beyond measure.

"The description of the boy seems to tally with yours," said Madam tersely, "and also that of the man who came to your office. Also, he sells patent medicine."

"Madam," said I, "this alarms me seriously."

"As well it may," she said, leaning forward so that the light fell upon her face, which had been in shadows.

"Madam!" I exclaimed, and arose abruptly to my feet.

"What is it, Orrin?" she asked solicitously.

I did not tell her, but the thing that had so startled me, was that, as Madam leaned forward and the light fell upon her features, I knew why the face of Gideon Weeks had seemed so familiar. For an instant the resemblance between Madam Janeway and Gideon Weeks was as the resemblance between twins.

She leaned back into the shadows and the impression passed. But it had been unmistakable.

She spoke sharply. "You have been placed on the alert," she said. Her eyes narrowed as she studied my face. "What action shall you take?"

"Madam," I said, "I shall make closer investigation."

She moved her hands impatiently. "Perhaps," she said, "Lossie's criticism of you was not unjust. You certainly do not leap without looking."

"I would not do an injustice," said I. "What would you have me do?"

I would not take my Bible oath to it, but it did seem to me that there was malice in her voice when she replied.

"Your duty as a citizen," she said inflexibly, "is to run the rascal out of town."

"Madam," I said, perhaps unwisely, "you speak as if the matter were of personal consequence to you."

"It is," she snapped, "as all law breaking—and especially clever frauds—is bound to be." She stood up imperiously in dismissal. "I hope, Orrin," she said more kindly, "that after you have slept on the matter you will agree with me what your course of action shall be."

I bowed and retired, but in a troubled state of mind. Oddly I wished I could lay the facts before Lossie and have her advice. I doubt if ever before I had considered her advice worth following.

$* \quad * \quad 8 \quad * \quad *$

I WALKED downtown after breakfast, worried about the situation that confronted me. On the way I passed the Bastable Building at Warren and Water Streets where the Cardiff Giant was being exhibited in a store. The rumor was traveling about that it was to be transported to Albany and exhibited in Geological Hall. I did not climb to my office, but continued on to the field on the outskirts of town where the medicine show was encamped. There I found a semimilitary encampment of which the large, ornate van was the center. Now the performers and employees were eating breakfast in an open-sided tent, and they did not seem to be the glamorous lot that displayed themselves to the public in the evening performances. Rather a sorry sight they presented, unshaven, in shirt sleeves or even not too immaculate flannel undershirts. The coffee, however, smelled good.

I approached the table at the head of which Gideon Weeks sat with his ham and eggs.

"Hey, rube!" someone called warningly as I approached, and a dozen heads turned in my direction with no welcome in any face.

"Mr. Weeks," I said, "may I speak with you?"

"Certainly, certainly, Applegate," he responded, and emptied his coffee cup at a draught. He threw his long legs over the wooden bench upon which he sat and strode toward me. He was a fine, upstanding body of a man, almost as tall as myself, but more neatly made.

"What," Weeks asked of me, extending a carefully tended hand, "brings you here so early in the morning?"

"We can," I said stoutly, "dispense with handshaking until we clear up a moot point."

His eyes narrowed and his lips formed a line under his mustache.

"Moot," he said. "Moot! That means a point about which there is an argument, doesn't it? Just what point is moot so early in the morning-o?"

I did not beat about the bush. "Your honesty," I said directly.

Weeks hunched his shoulders and doubled his fists, and I thought he was about to strike me, but I spoke quickly, "Hold your hosses," I warned. "I'm pretty stout, Mr. Weeks, and the canawlers have taught me how to rassle. I'd get the best of you."

He stopped and relaxed, and then grinned almost amiably. "Maybe you'd get the best of me, son, but what if I sicked the troupe onto you?"

"Why," I said, "I'd fight until I got licked, a dozen against one. And then I'd go down to the canal and collect my own dozen and demolish your troupe and your camp and leave the place a shambles."

He studied me a moment and shrugged. "I thought," he said, "that you were one of those James Street aristocrats."

"So I am," I told him, "but I ramify."

"Very good, Applegate, you ramify. You use words. You're a lawyer with book learning. You talk about moot. Now let's get down to this moot. What gives you the idea I'm not as honest as the sun that shines?"

"Well, Mr. Weeks," I said, "there's a sort of a freak of nature going around the country. It comes in the shape of a small boy who is endowed with a peculiar physical ability. He can disjoint himself at will. He can throw out his hips or his shoulders or his knees whenever he wants to. Which is a very handy thing if he wants to perpetrate a fraud. He can pretend to fall down somebody's stairs or to be hit by somebody's horses, and it looks like a genuine and severe injury. It even passes doctor's inspection because there is actual, visible dislocation. And he has a very good case for damages." I paused and fixed my eyes on his. "Is that moot enough for you, Mr. Weeks?"

He returned my gaze and quirked his head to one side and shrugged. "Just what steps do you intend to take, Mr. Applegate?"

"Why, first," said I, "I shall give you the opportunity to allow a committee of surgeons to verify the actuality of your boy's injuries. Following that, criminal prosecution will ensue."

"How old are you, Mr. Applegate?" he asked.

I did not see how it could concern him, but I told

him my age.

"For the life of me," he said admiringly, "I can't see how you could learn so much language in that many years." Then, becoming serious, he wrinkled his brow and narrowed his eyes and whistled through his teeth. "Sonny," he said patronizingly, "you didn't come up with this all by yourself. No young rube lawyer in this back country was ever that smart. I'll be obleeged to you, Mr. Applegate, if you'll tell me who put you wise."

"You're not denying?"

"Hell's floating rib, of course I'm not! I'm caught, so I'm caught. What's your proposition?"

"Clear out of town," I said firmly.

"No law?"

"Just clear out," I said.

He shrugged. "We got the place practically milked dry," he said. "I'd rather take my tarnation time pulling out than have to skedaddle between two days. But have it your way, Mr. Applegate; we vamoose."

"Twenty-four hours," I said.

"We'll head south. Frost's in the air. No hard feelings, sir. Come and have a cup of coffee with us. I'd like my folks to meet a smart rube lawyer."

He made a place beside him at the trestle table and a plate of ham and eggs and a tin cup of coffee were placed before me. Mr. Weeks appeared to hold no resentment, but, on the contrary, paid me compliments upon my astuteness and prophesied that one day I would be elevated to the Supreme Court. The small boy was brought out all properly jointed again. He seemed a stupid, mentally stunted child and I thought this might be due to the fact that he was nightly used as the mesmerist's subject. Much of the conversation was unintelligible to me, it being a sort of argot of the open road and of show business. A slim, weasel-faced, lugubrious man sat next to me and never moved a muscle of his face except to chew food.

Weeks indicated him to me. "He'd be the best conjurer in the nation," Weeks told me, "if only he had the patter to go with it. But he's practically dumb. But he's useful, Mr. Applegate. He's useful." He widened his eyes and peered at me humorously. "Now I warrant your wallet is full of money," he said, "and you've got a handkerchief in your back pocket and pencils in your vest and maybe a jackknife."

I felt for those articles, but my pockets were as empty as the day they came from the store.

"Give them back to our guest, Monk," Mr. Weeks said gaily, and the dour, skinny man passed back my belongings one by one without a glint of laughter in his dull eyes.

"If," said Weeks genially, "you want to learn things you never dreamt of, come and travel with us for a month. Human nature we'll teach you, and the work of nimble fingers, and the ease with which yokels can be made to bilk themselves. Sharpers, Mr. Applegate, don't have to be so sharp. It's the cupidity of people makes it easy for us. Smart Alecs trying to overreach us. Get something for nothing. Now, offhand, you might say, Mr. Applegate, that we played tricks on folks and maybe weren't a hundred per cent honest. But if there wasn't a broad streak of dishonesty in the crowds that come to see us, we'd have no luck. Come travel with us, Mr. Applegate. A couple of months on the road and you'll learn more than lawbooks can teach you in a year."

I was enjoying myself; of such frank rascality I never had dreamed. These people did not seem to me to be so much immoral as amoral. They lived by a different code from normal folks. They made no effort to justify themselves, but seemed to be convinced that they were merely holding their own in a dog-eat-dog world, and that there was no wrong in cheating somebody before that somebody could cheat them.

"But," I protested, "everybody in the world isn't trying to cheat everybody else. Syracuse is full of people of rectitude and integrity, living normal, honorable lives."

"To be sure," said Weeks. "Like those upstanding citizens who are making money hand over fist exhibiting a fake stone giant. I even hear rumors you had a murder here not so long ago."

"Some bad things happen among the canawlers," I said.

"This wasn't a canawler murder, the way I heard it. A stranger throttled and left in somebody's barn."

"Oh, that!" I said. "It was a dreadful thing. The victim was found in my father's barn, sitting in his carriage."

"And nobody," said Weeks, "has been arrested for it. Why not, Mr. Applegate? Somebody have influence?"

"No, indeed," I protested. "The dead man has not even been identified. No one in Syracuse ever had seen him alive."

"Somebody must have," Weeks said. "He didn't strangle himself, did he?"

"No. But he was exposed in the undertaking parlor as long as it was possible, and hundreds looked at him without identifying him."

"What kind of a looking hairpin was this feller?" asked the pickpocket, who sat next to me.

"A large, beefy man," I told him, "with burnside whiskers, kind of reddish color, and pale pop eyes."

"Dew tell," exclaimed the man with the deft fingers. "Naow he wouldn't maybe have had him on his right cheek a kind of a purple mole about the size of a sixpence?"

I sought to visualize the horrid face of that dead man as I had seen it in our carriage on the Sabbath morning. There was, indeed, if my memory served, a round discoloration on his cheek. "And another thing," I said, recollecting, "the second finger of one of his hands —I think it was the right—had been cut off at the second joint."

There was silence about that table—an ominous sort of silence. The members of the troupe looked at one another with narrowed, malicious eyes. Then, after a moment, all was as it had been.

Mr. Weeks shrugged. "For a moment," he said, "we thought it might be someone we knew."

"It was," mumbled the dull-witted boy. "I knowed

right off when he said about the cut-off finger. It was the Dook."

"Aw, shucks," said Mr. Weeks. "It couldn't have been."

"It was the Dook," reiterated the half-wit.

"All right," Weeks said after a moment. "It was the Duke. And if we didn't have to skedaddle out of town like we have, I'd make it my business to find out who treated our friend so."

"Me," said the slovenly girl who looked so lovely under the flaring lights at night, "I always said he'd come to a bad end. Always snoopin'. Always apryin'. Always tryin' to find out secrets. What I repeat is he come to the end I expected. He found out one secret too many."

"The Dook," said my light-fingered neighbor, "was a stout, heavy sort of a man. Anybody that hung onto him and throttled him with his hands would have to be stronger'n that feller that fit battles with the jawbone of an ass."

"Only man I know of stout enough to do that, 'n then hoist him into a carriage and set him down all neat and peaceful," declared the girl who sang ballads, "was Bigfoot Swede."

"If he done it," said the mesmerizer, "then I calc'late not to make it none of my business."

"Perhaps," said Weeks, "it is just as well we are moving south. . . . But Bigfoot's act did draw people to see our show."

"What," I asked, "was the Duke's real name?"

"Seems like I forget," Weeks said. "He was kind of

chary of mentioning it."

Weeks stood up politely and extended his hand to me. "It has been educational meeting you, Mr. Applegate," he said graciously. "I hope we meet sometime again."

After that I had to shake hands with all the members of the troupe, including the boy who could disjoint himself. And then I strolled back toward my office.

As I walked along, I had to face the fact that the most promising piece of law business that had come my way had blown up in my face and Lossie would laugh at me for being so thoroughly taken in by a scalawag. And I would have been taken in, had it not been for Madam Janeway and her warning. I might even have become an innocent party to a fraud and a sharer in its profits.

When I reached the building in which my office was located, I found a dray at the door on which was a modern safe of medium size. Pete Boss, the drayman, said he had thought I never would get there and that they had been waiting for an hour.

"But," I said, "I've bought no safe."

"That," Pete said, "is what you think. But here's the safe, all paid for, to be delivered to your office. Paid for in cash money by Madam Janeway."

There was nothing I could do about it. Maybe it was one of those lavish gifts for which Madame was so noted. Maybe she wanted me to have a safe for some reason of her own. I would call upon her at the first opportunity and find out. If it was a gift, then, of course,

I would decline to accept it. If, for some business reason, she wished to have a strongbox in my office, that would be a cat of another color.

"What's the combination?" I asked Pete.

"Me, I jest deliver. Don't know nothin' about combinations," he said.

I had my lunch downtown and spent a long afternoon in study and in waiting for clients to present themselves. At five o'clock I walked home. Again Lossie was raking leaves. I would have avoided her, but she pinned me down.

"And how," she asked, "is the burgeoning law practice today?"

"Big words!" I said. "Know what they mean?"

"You would be surprised half to death," she retorted, "if you knew what words I know, and other things."

"Ladylike, I hope."

"Useful anyhow," she said. "Are you going to take that damage case?"

"No," I told her. "Did you hang around and waylay me to find out?"

"Yes," she said promptly. "Why didn't you take it?"

"It was a fraud."

"So-o-o!" She drew out the word irritatingly. "And how would you recognize a fraud if you saw it?"

"I'm much smarter than you think," I said smugly.

"You're smart when somebody tells you how to be. What did Madam Cissie tell you last night?" Her voice was sharp, for which I could see no reason.

"If you must know," I told her, "Madam showed me a newspaper clipping about a boy who could disjoint himself whenever he wanted to."

"And how," she said, still tartly, "did Madam happen to have such a clipping handy?"

"She has a scrapbook," I said. "In it she keeps pieces about clever crimes."

"Oh-ho! And what did you do about it?"

"I told these medicine-show people to vamoose out of town."

"Was that your own idea?" she asked.

"Anyhow they're clearing out. And I admit I sort of liked them. Scalawags or not, I liked them."

She gave quick, little, jerky nods of her head. "Then the day wasn't wasted," she said. "You're improving."

"Also," said I a bit boastfully, "I found out something all the police in Syracuse have missed."

"My, what a long tail our cat has got!" she jeered.

"I found out the identity of that murdered man in our barn."

"Why, Mr. Pinkerton!" she exclaimed. "Who was he?"

"A man," I told her, "named the Duke."

"That makes everything clear. A medicine-show man?"

"Yes," I said. "They think he was strangled by another man they know, called Bigfoot Swede."

"And what, Mr. Pinkerton, do you propose to do with this knowledge?"

"Keep it to myself while I think it over."

She blinked at me. "Little playmate," she said, "if I were you I'd keep it to myself longer than that. I'd tie a stone around it and sink it in oblivion. At this exact minute, Orrin, I would estimate that it is the most dangerous bit of knowledge existing in Syracuse."

* * 9 * *

IT was midmorning of a crisp November day when Madam Janeway, accompanied by Lossie Fox, rapped on the door of my law office and came in to sit down in my two chairs. Two lovelier women never graced a room. Madam's beauty was that of dignity and graciousness and maturity; Lossie's loveliness was what, or so I have heard, the French people describe as *beauté du diable*. Which, I am told, does not mean what it seems to signify.

"Orrin," Madam said, resting her slender gloved hand on the arm of her chair, "this is not exactly law business that I have come about, yet I would be gratified if, as my representative, you would handle the details." She smiled almost shyly. "I'm a poor manager, sir."

"How may I serve you?" I asked, and Lossie wrinkled her nose in derision of my formality.

"There is much distress in this city," Madam said. "People are cold and hungry."

"There is," I answered, "distress all over the nation." Which was true. We were in the midst of the most severe hard times the country had experienced since the

124

great Panic of 1857. Banks had toppled, business houses were bankrupt, unemployment was severe, and the end was not in sight. People blamed it upon the manipulations of men like Gould and Dan'l Drew and Jim Fisk. Perhaps they were right.

"On Thanksgiving Day," said Madam, "it would pleasure me to feed the hungry."

"All of them?" I asked in astonishment.

"All who care to come," she said.

"But, Madam," I expostulated, "there will be thousands."

She nodded. "I estimate," she said briskly, "that we shall require five thousand loaves of bread. At least three large beeves must be barbecued and we must have an immense amount of plum pudding. We must have the permission of the city authorities to use Clinton Square. There will have to be stands for music, tables, fences to hold the crowd in order. There will have to be wood for the roasting ovens."

"Madam is an organizer!" Lossie said innocently.

"You, Orrin," said Madam succinctly, "will examine the various bills and approve them with your signature. Mr. Watts will then pay them at the bank. We have only two weeks to perfect the arrangements."

Madam had been quiescent for some time, almost in retirement, but now she was emerging with a vengeance. All her benefactions, all her gifts, all her entertainments of the past paled into nothingness when compared to this thing that she proposed.

"Madam," I exclaimed, "this will be a sensation.

Nothing like it ever has been done before. There will be notoriety; perhaps more than you have foreseen. From which a fastidious lady may shrink."

It was Lossie who replied, her level eyes fixed upon mine with an expression which I could not fathom. "Orrin," she said, "you are wrong to try to daunt Madam. Her mind is made up to do this charity. Hateful as the notoriety may be, Madam will endure it." I could have sworn that her left eye quivered. If she had been less demure and dignified as she sat there, I should have called it a hoydenish wink! She reached out her hand and touched Madam's fingers. "Who was that Greek philosopher who founded the stoics? Zeno? Well, Madam, I'm sure, is prepared to be a disciple of his. Aren't you, Madam?"

Madam Janeway shrugged. "I suppose a modicum of notoriety is unavoidable," she said resignedly.

"By the way, Madam," I said, "that safe!" I pointed to the strongbox which she had caused to be delivered to my office.

"Oh, that," she said with a shrug. "I thought it might come in handy. You don't mind, do you? A lawyer should have a safe to keep the private papers of his clients secure."

"True," I said, "provided he is the custodian of private papers." I paused and smiled. "But without the combination it is quite useless."

"You haven't the combination?" she exclaimed.

"It was not given to me," I told her.

"How extraordinary," she said, and rose. The combination was not given to me nor was it again referred to. She returned to the subject of the barbecue. "You will commence making plans," she said imperatively.

"At once," I told her. She took my hand and pressed it.

I opened the door and she passed out into the hall. Lossie was about to follow, but uttered an exclamation and turned back into the office. There she picked up the reticule she had dropped on the floor. As she straightened up she twinkled her eyes at me.

"There's another kind of Greek philosophy and I don't know who invented it," she said.

"Which one is that?" I asked.

"I think," she said with gravity, "that they called it cynicism."

After they were gone I made some notes, and then, putting on my overcoat, I went out to lay Madam's project before the city authorities and get their permission to use Clinton Square for the barbecue. My request was taken under advisement. Then I walked briskly along to a market where I could inquire about the three large beeves necessary to the feeding.

As I came out of this place of business, I looked across the basin, and there, made fast securely, was Lizzie Ann. She was not merely secured there as she would have been if she were soon to be on her way again along the canal; she was really made fast with strong ropes in a manner that told me she was tied up for the winter. It was time. Already in the mornings there was thin ice on the surface of the water. It was the season for the first big freeze which would halt all traffic on Governor Clinton's Ditch until the coming of spring and the melting of the ice. Not until late March or early April would the boats be able again to ply that great waterway that connected the Hudson River with the Great Lakes.

It was a curious thing that I, Orrin Applegate, raised as I had been, and inhibited as I had been by the mores of my parents and Lossie's parents and our neighbors, should have felt so completely at home with Zacharias Wheelright and his woman. Of course I never would have known them had it not been for Lossie and her complete lack of inhibitions when she was a little girl. It was she who had come to love these two canawlers first, and then, in spite of myself, I had come to love their simplicity and kindness and wisdom on my own account. For they were wise, both of them. Zacharias was wise in a placid way that fitted his bigness. Ma Wheelright, as she delighted to hear us call her, was wise in a pert, birdlike way that constantly used unorthodox but original expressions and saws and homemade epigrams. This in spite of the fact that upon one point only was she, as the canawlers were wont to say, "a bit tetched." The point was that she seemed to believe Lossie was her dead daughter, and always spoke to her and treated her as such. Unlettered they both were, but possessed of what Ma Wheelright referred to as "mother wit." If I ever stood in need of practical advice, I am sure I would have gone to them before I would have appealed to the Chief Justice of the Supreme Court.

I walked to the bridge and crossed the canal to reach the spot where Lizzie Ann was tied and, sure of a welcome, I stepped aboard and called, "Hey, below there! Uncle Zach! Maw Wheelright!"

The great golden head and spreading golden beard of Zacharias Wheelright appeared, and his big sky-blue eyes were alight with welcome.

"Woman," he called in a voice like that of the Bull of Bashan, "it's Orrin! Sure's all git out it's Orrin come to see us!"

"Tell the scamp to come moggin' right daown!" Maw Wheelright called in her brisk, cackling voice. "The's fresh-made ginger cookies. . . . Where's Lizzie Ann, boy? Why didn't you fetch her along?"

"Just saw you tied up," I said. I pushed my way past Zach's bulk and hoisted Maw's thin body in my arms to kiss her resoundingly.

"Goodness gracious!" she said nasally. "Every time ye git bigger. Most as big as Zach, I declare. Put me daown, you spriggins. Put me daown."

"Calc'late to winter here," Zach said. "Mebby I'll contrive to let out the team to loggers or somebuddy. Mebby I'll take a job myself."

"Ye don't need to, ye ol' skeezicks," Maw said snappishly. "We got ample in the ol' teapot to winter us. And I don't cater none to bein' left alone whilst ye hyper off into the woods."

"To be sure, woman," Zach replied. "But me, I can't abide wearin' thin the seat of my pants in idleness."

It was warm and comfortable there, and serene,

but I could not linger. I told them I must get along and attend to business, and Maw said not to get too big for my britches because I was a lawyer now. I promised to bring Lossie that afternoon and took my departure.

"I'm mullin' over in my mind," Zach said as I stood on the wall, "whether to keep things to myself or repeat rumors that come to me."

I knew it would be of no avail to urge him. He would talk when he was ready, if ever. The canal was alive with facts and rumors and gossip which never reached the outside world. How the commonwealth of canawlers learned so much will always remain a mystery to me, and how they kept to themselves secrets that would have rocked communities or even the state itself was a miracle.

"When you're ready, Uncle Zach," I said, "I'll listen."

Maw screamed from the cabin, "The'll be a brewin' of tea around four o'clock!"

I did what I could to make arrangements for Madam Janeway's barbecue, and when there was nothing more I could accomplish that day I walked home to tell Lossie the Lizzie Ann was in the basin and see if she wanted to go down and visit our friends. I whistled our whistle and she flattened her nose against the windowpane. I motioned for her to come out, which she did in five minutes. She could have come in one, but felt it was necessary to keep me waiting in the cold.

"We have a doorbell," she said primly.

"Doorbells," I said, "are for strangers."

"Would you," she demanded, "stand outside and whistle for Madam Janeway?"

"I didn't rock Madam's cradle when she was a month old," I retorted.

She stood off a little way and turned around in a small circle. "Look at me, Orrin Applegate," she commanded. "Am I grown up or am I not grown up?"

"Grown up or not grown up," I said stubbornly, "you are Lossie."

She stomped her little foot. "I won't have it so!" she said furiously. "I will be treated with respect! I will be treated as a lady!"

She was standing on the front stoop, which was four steps high and surrounded by a railing. At its side was a freshly heaped pile of dry maple leaves.

I spoke quickly, urgently. "Double dare you," I said, "to jump off the rail into that pile."

What followed was reflex. Lossie scrambled to the top of the rail, gathered up her dignified skirts and leaped. The air was full of lovely, slender legs and billowing skirts, and she landed in a breathless heap, half buried by the leaves. I reached for a hand and jerked her erect and grinned as irritatingly as I could manage.

"Tomboy," I said jeeringly.

I was ready to defend myself, but there was no wildcat attack such as I had learned to expect. Instead she turned pale and bit her lips, and then she flushed and seemed on the point of crying, so that I was ashamed of myself and contrite. But before I could humiliate myself to her and make my peace, she burst into gay laughter and kicked the leaves in all directions and took me by the arm like the Lossie of ten years ago and said with a little pout, "Anyhow"—and her voice was merry— "anyhow I'm grown up some of the time."

"Lizzie Ann is in," I told her, "and there'll be tea and ginger cookies."

"Oh, let's hurry," she said, and gave me a push. "We'll cut across lots."

Cutting across lots was a local custom. We did not regard it as trespass. So, instead of walking down James Street, we crossed to walk through Madam Janeway's property to the lane behind. We walked on the grass heading for the gate at the end of the barn. Our way carried us past the window of the room that Madam used as her office. We heard a voice harsh with anger. It came distinctly through the upraised window and it halted us. On our part was no intention to eavesdrop, but we were startled to motionlessness and stood there as if frozen. There was fury and venom in the voice. It was the hoarse, harsh voice of Oscar, the butler. He was profane and unrestrained.

"You damn peacock!" he said. "You show-off! You want to ruin us! You want to ruin everything! Not the common sense God gave geese!"

He seemed to splutter and choke, and Madam's voice, low and frightened, expostulated, "But, Oscar——"

"Be still!" he shouted. "Your damn vanity! You got to make a parade! Charity, sure! Fool generosity! Cause talk! And now this—this damn lunacy! I've a mind to wring your neck!"

"But, Oscar—Oscar——" Madam pleaded.

Lossie looked at me with something like horror in her eyes, and I peered back, shocked and amazed.

"We better," I said in a whisper, "get out of here."

"And fast," Lossie replied. "And quietly."

We went away from there both fast and quietly, and it was not until we were a full block away that we spoke again.

Then it was Lossie who asked breathlessly, "Orrin, what did that mean?"

I shook my head. "Oscar doesn't approve of Madam's barbecue."

"But—but what right has he to disapprove? To speak to her so?"

I could only shake my head. "Let's hurry to Lizzie Ann," I said in a sort of desperation. "Lizzie Ann, where all who are on her are clean."

As we passed the Bastable Building the store door was open and we could see men straining to hoist the great weight of the Cardiff Giant into a strong crate for shipping to Albany. The new owners of it openly boasted that after they had refused to sell it to the great showman, P. T. Barnum, that gentleman had offered them sixty thousand dollars to rent it to him for three months.

We walked with heavy feet, Lossie and I, down to the basin and Lizzie Ann.

"Lossie," I said, "how would a servant dare to

speak so to a great lady like Madam Janeway?"

"His manner," Lossie said, "was more that of a master than of a servant!" There came a little pause. "He was afraid," she said.

"Afraid!" I exclaimed. "It was she who was frightened!"

She shook her head. "Men fly into that sort of rage," she said positively, "only when they are scared."

"But why should he be afraid? Why should her barbecue frighten him into such a rage?"

"That much," she said promptly, "was clear enough. It was because she called attention to herself. Because of the display. Because it would get her talked about."

"But," I said, "almost everything she does gets her talked about. She likes to be talked about. Even if she did none of the things she does—her entertainments, her gifts, her charities—she would be conspicuous. Her beauty. The way she lives. Those whispers about Dan'l Drew."

Lossie spoke to herself as if she were protesting, arguing against some conclusion that vexed her. "But," she said insistently, "she is kind. She is generous. She is charitable. She does sympathize with misfortunes."

"Can it be," I asked, "that this Oscar objects to the lavish way she throws money about? That, in addition to being her butler, he is also a sort of business manager?"

"No," Lossie said. "A businessman might be exasperated. He might protest and argue. He wouldn't fly into a murderous temper. It was because this display endangers something. Didn't you see that, Orrin? Endangers something. Some plan."

"What plan could he be up to?" I demanded.

"How should I know?" she retorted. "But he's compelling her to help with it. He has some way to compel her."

"It doesn't make sense," I objected. "Madam is rich and highly connected. Why, Lossie, she has hundreds and hundreds of thousands of dollars' worth of securities. I've seen them."

"It's contradictory," Lossie said slowly. "If there's some sort of scheme, then it was necessary for Madam to set the river on fire. She had to astonish the town. She had to be a nine days' wonder. And then this Oscar flies into an insane temper because she thinks up the most extravagant caper of all!"

"The one thing that is clear to me," I said gravely, "is that Madam is in this Oscar's power."

"Like in a melodrama," Lossie said, jeering at me.

"Like in a melodrama," I said firmly.

"And so," she said, with a sudden change of attitude and with testiness in her voice, "the hero will fly to the aid of the heroine."

"I am her lawyer," I said.

"To what," she demanded, "does that entitle her?"

I thought that question over and it was not simple to answer. She paid me a retainer, a regular sum of money monthly. That entitled her to call upon me for any reasonable legal service that was ethical or within the law. It entitled her to my loyalty and to my best efforts in her behalf, if called upon.

Lossie had an uncanny way of following my thoughts. "But, Orrin," she asked, "does your retainer entitle her to have you dive in when you don't know how deep it is? Does it require you to volunteer? To stick in your big nose before you're asked?"

"As an officer of the court," I said a bit pompously, "I would be required to take action if I became aware of a wrong or a crime."

"Cock-a-doodle-do!" Lossie jeered. "And just what wickedness have you uncovered, Mr. Officer of the Court?"

"Why," said I after reflection, "none, I guess. Only a disturbing and bewildering state of affairs."

"Which neither of us understands?"

"Which," I agreed, "neither of us understands."

"There are a heap of axioms in the law, aren't there?" she asked.

"Hundreds," I answered.

"All right, Mr. Smug," she said. "Here's a new one. I just invented it. 'When bewildered, keep your mouth shut and your ears and eyes open.' How's that?"

"Here's another one," I said promptly. " 'If you can't tell which is right and which is wrong, then do as you would be done by and hope for the best.' "

She studied me a moment and nodded her head in agreement. "With the accent," she said, "on 'hope for the best.' "

We reached the canal and crossed the bridge. It was not far down the towpath to the basin and Lizzie Ann. The huge body of Zacharias sat on the after rail and he was puffing placidly on his pipe. His big blue eyes above his bristling golden whiskers did not seem to see us, but as we came abreast he lifted his voice in a bellow.

"Woman," he shouted so it could be heard down the reaches of the canal, "they've come!"

With which he reached down and swung Lossie aboard as if she had no more weight than a feather, and held her aloft so that he could look into her lovely flushed face.

"If," she said contentedly, "I could wade through your beard I'd give you a big kiss."

"Aim for my nose," Zach said delightedly. "My mouth's jest underneath it."

"You put that child down and demean yourself," snapped a nasal voice from the hatchway. "You hyper right daown here, Lizzie Ann, and give your ma a smack."

It was warm and cozy in the cabin, and there was the pleasant odor of baking and of maple burning in the cookstove. One could not imagine a higher state of cleanliness, and Maw Wheelright was as neat as the cozy room, with hair tightly combed and twisted into a bun on top of her head. She bustled. Even when she sat still in her rocker she seemed to be bustling. In spite of her years, she was the most alive person I ever knew.

"Ye look right peart, darlin', what with the frost on your cheeks," she said comfortably. "The purtiest age," she added, "is jest when a gal's comin' to life and hain't yit aware of what's happenin' to her. . . . What's vexin' you 'n' her, Orrin? Had a spat?"

"No spat, Maw Wheelright," I replied. "We're just worried."

"If," Zach's woman said, "ye hain't obleeged to keep shet about it, then ye fetched it to the right place. Zach's got the muscles and I got the mother wit."

Zach was amused. "Yup," he said fondly, "and ye got what turned Lot's wife into a bag of salt."

"When I was here earlier today," I said to him, "you told me there was talk along the canal. That you might be willing to tell me about."

"I hear tell," Zacharias said, apparently avoiding the question, "that ye run a medicine show out of taown."

"It should be gone by this time," I answered.

"Ye ketched 'em aworkin' that disjointin' caper with the boy?"

"Yes," I told him.

"They been afollerin' the canal along from Albany, mostly gittin' hauled from place to place on canal boats. So they kind of come to our attention."

"They would be noticed," I agreed.

"When two, three boats ties up together fur the night," Zach said, "the's gossipin'."

"Like a passel of crows congregatin' in a hick'ry tree," interjected Maw Wheelright. "Canawlers talks to canawlers. But this here medicine troupe lickered up and talked to anybuddy."

"So," said Zach, "we come by the knowledge that they wan't jest atravelin' 'n' sellin' their remedies 'n' tendin' to their other normal business, like pickin' pockets. But they was seekin' somebuddy."

"I think I know," I said. "A man who was strangled and put in our barn."

Zach shook his head. "That hadn't happened yit," he said. "Nay! 'Twan't that murdered man they was aseekin'. From what we pieced together, here 'n' there, we calc'lated it was a female. We kind of come to the conclusion she jumped ship daown in Pennsylvania 'n' gobbled up all the money was in the box. Quite a sum they'd took in durin' a favorable season."

"After that," Zach's woman said, "seems like they couldn't hold the show together. Not big as it used to be."

"Some performers skedaddled," said Zach. "A knife-throwin' artist 'n' another they called the Dook 'n' others."

"Who," I told him, "was the murdered man we found in our barn."

"Dew tell!" Zach exclaimed.

"Them," said Zach's woman, "that live by the sword shall die by the sword."

" 'Twan't a sword killed him, woman," Zach said; "it was stranglin'."

"Ye was of a mind to git our advice about suthin," said Maw Wheelright. "Naow's a fit time to ask it."

She rose and lifted the pot from the stove and poured its aromatic contents into four cups. From the cupboard she took a great plate of ginger cookies and fat, sugared white cookies.

"Growin' children," she said, "should eat frequent."

Lossie and I moved up to the table. It was growing dark and outside could be heard the whistling of a northwest wind which was likely to bring snow. The Lizzie Ann was motionless, not stirred by the gale, because the thickening ice held her firmly.

While we munched cookies and drank scalding tea there was no conversation, just comfort and companionship. Then there came the sudden trampling of heavy feet on the deck above and a rasping voice called down the hatchway, "You, Applegate! If you're down there, come up!"

Zach stood up, his big blue eyes narrowing.

"Sounds hostile," said his woman. "Better see who, Zach."

His big frame mounted the steps until his head appeared above deck.

"Who be you," he asked in his great voice, "and what's wanted?"

"We want Applegate," said the same unpleasant voice.

Zach climbed through the opening and stood on deck. I followed him and stood at his side. Confronting us were nigh onto a dozen men, and in the twilight I recognized them as members of the Umatilla Indian patent-medicine troupe. Some were performers, others teamsters or laborers of some sort. But tall, handsome Gideon Weeks was not among them.

"What," I asked, "are you doing in town yet? What do you want with me?"

"We come," grated the pickpocket, "to do to you

like you done to Gideon Weeks."

"And what," I demanded, "did I do to Gideon Weeks?"

"You wrung his neck!" yelled the man beside the pickpocket, and he leaped for me.

It was somewhat of a battle before it ended. There were several of them, and only Zacharias Wheelright and I. But the space was narrow and we were not of negligible size. I heard Zach bellow and then I was busy. My fists whacked against bone, and fists struck at me. Out of the corner of my eye I saw Zach lift the pickpocket in his mighty arms and hurl him at his companions. A man tried to grasp my legs, but I kicked him in the chest and that was all for him. They gave back and we moved forward, and presently what was left of them turned tail and ran. But four or five remained prone or writhing in agony. I hoisted one of the latter to his feet and shook him.

"Now," I demanded, "what's the meaning of this?"

"He's dead with his neck twisted," the man whined. "Weeks is dead, and you done it."

"Throttled?" I asked.

"Neck twisted like a chicken's."

"Why," I demanded, shaking the fellow vigorously, "do you think I killed him?"

"Stands to reason," the man whimpered. "Killed the Dook, didn't ye? In your barn. Same way. Ye was runnin' Weeks out of taown. Mebby he didn't skedaddle quick enough."

I tossed the creature to the deck. "We'd better call

the police," I said to Zacharias Wheelright.

"What fur?" Zach demanded. "Calc'late these'll be able to walk away by themselves. I don't favor dealin' with the police."

"That's right, Orrin," piped up Zach's woman. "Least said soonest mended."

Lossie spoke then, almost for the first time since we came aboard, and there was something in her eyes I never had seen before. She did not jeer at me nor belittle me. Her fingers bit into my arm. "Goodness gracious," she exclaimed in a little girl's voice, "but you're a dandy fighter!"

"Him 'n' Zach," said his woman in her high, metallic voice, "is a pair. Come back daown 'n' finish your piece."

We went back down into the warmth of the cabin and Maw Wheelright replenished our cups.

"But who killed Mr. Weeks? And why?" I asked aloud.

"Somebuddy," Maw replied, "that prefers fingers to weepons."

"The same one," Lossie added, "who throttled the Duke."

I was uncomfortable about the whole business; I mean that it had happened while Lossie was there to be a part of it. Certainly it had been no place for a lady.

"Lossie," I accused myself, "I got you into this mess."

She grinned up at me like a naughty urchin and made a curtsy. "Mr. Applegate," she said, "if you got me into more messes like this one, I'd stick to you tighter than a bur."

Maw Wheelright was bobbing her head and her little eyes were twinkling.

"Boy," she said, "Lossie got you into plenty mischief when you was children. It's high time ye done the same by her now you've growed up."

Lossie shook her head. "He'd never do it by himself," she said. "I have to inveigle him."

* * 10 * *

BECAUSE Gideon Weeks was a low person, a
kind of tramp, and with a medicine show, the authorities
made very little fuss about his death. His troupe had no
desire to be mixed up with the law, but only wanted to
get out of town as quickly as possible. So there was an
end of it so far as I was concerned, and my name never
came up. But those Umatilla people held a grudge against
me, as was but natural. However, they scattered. It was
the end of the show. They sold their horses and left their
van in a lot by the livery barn and took themselves away.

I was very busy with the arrangements for Madam
Janeway's barbecue. The authorities gave permission to
have the affair in Clinton Square. When the account of it
appeared in the papers, it caused a great deal of excitement, not only in Syracuse but as far away as Albany
and New York, for it appeared that nobody ever had
planned that sort of thing for charity before, and certainly never on so huge a scale. If Madam desired to be
talked about, she certainly won her heart's desire. There
were chalkplate portraits of her in papers as far away as
Boston and Brooklyn, which, I must say, resembled her

very little. Certainly no one would have recognized her from these caricatures.

She spent hours in my office, and Lossie came along with her. I must say that Madam had a genius for planning and making arrangements. All I had to do was to carry out, to the best of my ability, her directions. On the appointed day all was ready, and Syracuse was agog. The indigent, who were to be the beneficiaries of Madam's bounty, were massed in one place and there restrained until the signal for their rush should be given.

North of the canal I had caused to be erected a platform twenty feet square upon which were stacked five thousand loaves of bread. This was flanked by roasting ovens and piles of split wood to feed them. There was a table at the north a hundred feet long, and a bandstand and a reviewing stand for notables. It might have meant food to the hungry, but to others it was an amazing spectacle. I estimated that twenty thousand people from town or from the surrounding country crowded all space left available for spectators. They jammed windows overlooking the square and occupied roofs high above the street. Half a dozen excursion trains brought holidaymaking crowds to the city.

At half past ten on that beautiful morning the signal was given and the beneficiaries of the feast were turned loose to rush in a body upon the great pile of bread and the roasted meat. It was nearly a riot, and it continued until midafternoon, when the throng dwindled and only the debris of the sensational barbecue remained to be cleaned up and disposed of.

It had been a tremendous success. Madam Janeway's name was on every tongue, either in praise and friendship, or in jealousy and malice. But to me the strangest phenomenon of the day was the invisibility of the benefactress. She was not present. She did not gratify her eyes by watching the event. It was not like her. I would have expected her to be much in evidence, basking in the applause, delighting in the excitement and the cheers and the publicity of it. But from morning until night she concealed herself. It was not modesty. Knowing Madam as I did, associating with her as I had done, I was positive that nothing could have kept her away save dire illness or physical force.

When half the day had elapsed without her appearance, I felt it my duty to seek the reason for it. So I withdrew from the great crowd and hastened to her house across the street from Lossie's and my own.

I rang the bell. It was unanswered. I pounded on the side door to no avail; nor did I have better fortune at the kitchen door. From inside came neither sound nor movement. Doors and windows were securely locked. In the barn the handsome team of horses trampled and munched in their stalls. The coachman snored in his room. I awakened him.

"Where is everybody?" I demanded. "Where is Madam?"

He looked up at me with sleep-bleared eyes. "Dunno, Mr. Applegate," he said. "Hain't seed hide nor hair of any of 'em all day."

I returned to Clinton Square to supervise the cleaning up, and then hurried home in time for supper. I was confronted by a mystery. I was nonplused and apprehensive.

Lossie must have been watching for me in her front window, for she came to the door and called to me. I walked to the foot of the steps and waited for her to speak.

"Chores finished?" she asked.

"All I can do until tomorrow."

She leaned her slender shoulder against a post. "Worried?" she asked.

"Why should I be?" I countered.

"I would be if I were you," she said.

"Why would you be worried?"

"Her lawyer, aren't you?"

"You know I am."

"If," she said, "I were a lawyer and my best client, who is the vainest woman in the world, failed to appear on the day most likely to tickle her vanity, I'd be pretty startled."

"I am, Lossie," I said frankly.

"I saw you trying to get into her house," she said.

"Not a soul there."

Lossie settled her shawl about her shoulders and sat down on the top step, patting the place beside her in invitation. I sat down and rested my head on my fists.

"She wouldn't have missed all the hullabaloo willingly," Lossie said.

"No," I agreed. "Not willingly."

"I'm thinking," Lossie said, "about what we over-heard."

"Madam and Oscar?"

"His rage about this barbecue," she said.

"It was rage, Lossie," I said, "but it was also some-thing else. It was fear."

She nodded. "Afraid," she said, "of Madam's call-ing attention to herself in such a big way."

I nodded unhappily. "So he hid her away so strangers coming to town couldn't see her."

Lossie agreed with me. "It could be nothing else," she said. She sat in moody silence for a minute and then she turned to me. "But Madam is kind," she protested, as if someone had denied it. "She's generous. She loves to give. She sympathizes with the unfortunate. Those things are real."

"You would know better than I." Then, after a pause, "But why should Oscar be afraid of notoriety? What right had he to be afraid of notoriety? Just a servant."

"A knife-throwing servant," Lossie said softly.

"It's a strange relationship," I said.

"Only you and I know about it," Lossie said, with a wrinkle between her eyes.

"He has," I said, "some way of making Madam obey him." I thought about that phase of the matter. "He could," I said, "be a criminal who has got a hold on her and means to rob her of her money."

"Is she really rich, Orrin?"

"I think she is very rich," I said. "I've seen thick packages of stocks and bonds. I know she has deposited some of them with Banker Watts and with that fawning little Jethro Willis over at Binghamton."

"Why would she deposit them with bankers?"

"For safekeeping," I explained. "We know she is highly connected."

"How do we know?" Lossie asked. "Did she ever say so?"

"Not in my hearing. But Banker Watts knows about it or he would not have stood as her sponsor in Syracuse."

"What relation is she to Dan'l Drew, the millionaire?"

"Mr. Watts must know, and Jethro Willis, and Horatio Dewitt over in Albany. I've never heard her mention him. But they must know. It seems sure he does things for her—not little things, but up in the hundreds of thousands."

Lossie pondered. "Most folks think she is his illegitimate daughter," she said. "Do you think Oscar is trying to steal her money?"

"That might be difficult," I said. "If her wealth is in stocks and bonds and in her name, Oscar couldn't negotiate them."

"Unless," Lossie said, "he could compel her to sign her name to them—or if he were a forger and signed her name so it couldn't be detected."

"Yes."

"Orrin," Lossie said, and her voice was strained

with apprehension, "two people have been murdered since Madam came to town."

"Medicine-show people," I answered. "If not criminals, then on the fringe. There could be no connection with Madam Janeway."

"Was Oscar a medicine-show performer," she asked, "and maybe a member of this same troupe?"

"That," I said, "we do not know."

"But we suspect," she said. "Orrin," she asked worriedly, "has Madam Janeway ever asked you, as her attorney, to do anything that—that disturbed you?"

"You mean that was unethical?"

"I mean," she said, "that could get you into trouble."

"Never," I said positively.

"Has she ever given you the combination to that safe she had placed in your office?"

"No," I told her. "There's been no reason for it. So far as I know, the safe is empty."

"Do you know that we two are the only ones in all Syracuse who suspect something is wrong in that house across the way?"

"I suppose we are," I answered uncomfortably.

"I just most particularly hope," she said, "that Oscar doesn't find out about us. Or, for the matter of that, Madam Janeway."

"Nonsense," I said sharply.

"Didn't those medicine-show people tell you the Duke was a snoop?" she asked. "And maybe died because of it?"

"Gideon Weeks intimated as much."

"Could it be—could it possibly be that Mr. Weeks was a snoop also? And died of snooping?"

"I suppose it is possible. There must have been a reason of some sort."

"I'd think so," she said, and rather hastily added, "I don't think one man would throttle another just to exercise his fingers."

"What a thing to say!" I rebuked her. "Not lady-like."

"I wish," she said pettishly, "your mother never had given you that Book of Decorum for Christmas. Why can't you imitate Colonel Ingersoll and be an agnostic about it?"

"About a book of decorum!"

"Certainly," she said. "If he can have doubts about the truth of things in the Bible, you could be agnostic enough to think that some of those rules of good manners and behavior are all stuff and nonsense. Which," she said, clapping her hands together, "they most certainly are."

"Lossie Fox," I said, "what would happen if your mother heard you talk like that?"

"She," said Lossie, "would blow up and bust. Oh, I wish I were a canawler."

"So you could be positively lawless?" I asked.

"And not have a smidgin of manners," she said.

"Canawlers!" I exclaimed. And then, "But, Lossie, Captain Zacharias Wheelright and his woman have very fine and gentle manners."

"They didn't get them out of a book!" she snapped.

Which was true. The gentleness and consideration which Zach Wheelright and his woman showed at all times and on all occasions never were learned from the printed page.

"Come on in to supper," Lossie invited suddenly. "We got partridges and mince pie."

"Sure you got enough?" I asked.

"If you don't make a pig of yourself," she told me. "Go tell your mother and I'll tell the cook."

I went home and washed and shaved and put on clean linen and crossed to Lossie's house, which I entered without knocking, as I had done ever since I could walk. I hung my coat and hat on the black-walnut hall tree and was about to step into the back parlor. But Lossie called to me from the front parlor, which was in darkness. Dimly I could see her kneeling before the big window with its lace curtains pushed aside.

"Look," she said, and made room for me.

I looked across the street. Lights were coming on, one by one, in Madam Janeway's residence until it became a blaze of light. I saw Oscar draw the shades in the library, but could see into Madam's bedroom on the second floor. Madam stood there before her dresser, staring into the wide mirror. Suddenly, startlingly, she picked up a statuette and with all her strength hurled it into the looking glass, shattering it into a thousand pieces.

Lossie nudged me. "Something," she said mischievously, "has made Madam lose her temper."

"Pull down that shade," I commanded, "and stop snooping."

"That would be best," she said with an impish grin. She felt of her slender neck and made a face at me. "Throttling isn't a death I covet."

Mrs. Fox's voice called to us. "Children," she bade, "come sit down. Supper's ready."

* * 11 * *

MR. David Hannum, one of the syndicate who owned the Cardiff Giant, came into my office with a gentleman whom I never had seen before, but who was introduced to me as Colonel Wood, a professional show-man. This individual was to have charge of exhibiting the giant in various cities throughout the country. Both men were angry and disturbed.

"Orrin," Mr. Hannum said, "we want ye should git out an injunction agin P. T. Barnum."

"To stop him," I asked, "from doing what?"

"Exhibitin' an imitation of our giant," Mr. Hannum said. "I hear tell he's hired a sculptor to carve out a statue to be as like ourn as two peas, which he aims to exhibit in his museum on Broadway as the Cardiff Giant."

"Are you sure of your facts?" I asked.

"Dead sartin, Orrin."

"Mr. Hannum," I said gravely, "I fear you will fall afoul of a legal maxim, sir."

"Sich as?" demanded the banker and horse trader.

"He who comes into a court of equity must come

with clean hands," I said impressively.

Mr. Hannum examined his horny, callused paws and squinted at me under the peak of his cap. "Look tol'able washed to me," he said.

"I was not referring to physical cleanliness, but to ethical cleanliness."

"Meanin' jest what, young feller?"

"Are you prepared to prove that the Cardiff Giant is actually a petrified human being, as advertised?"

"Is anybuddy," he countered, "in a position to prove it hain't?"

"I question," said I, "if the courts will entertain an action to compel Mr. Barnum to cease and desist from exhibiting an imitation of a humbug."

Mr. Hannum fixed me with his shrewd, beady eyes. "Supposin' our giant is a humbug," he said. "Which I don't no ways admit. We had ourn fust, didn't we? Don't that create no rights?"

I gave the problem thought. "Why," I said after a time, "if Mr. Barnum should exhibit his giant and advertise it as the original Cardiff Giant, an action might lie."

"Good enough fur me," Hannum said. "You git the papers ready and start to whizzin'. We're atakin' our giant to New York in a couple of weeks. Yup. We've rented a store not two blocks from Barnum's Museum."

"Mr. Hannum," I said in my most dignified manner, "it is well for a client to be absolutely truthful with his lawyer. Do you believe your giant to be a veritable petrified monster, a statue of great antiquity, or a fraud?"

His reply was characteristic. "Some says one way, some says another," he told me. "Naow take Perfessor Alexander McWhorter—him that teaches in Yale College Divinity School."

"Yes?" I said.

"He claims," said Hannum, "that it's turrible ancient, and was wrought by them old Phoenicians. He claims the's a Bible-times inscription to be deciphered onto it. An' take Perfessor White, of Yale Medical School. What's he declare? He examined it with what he calls an achromatic glass, which sounds to me like a durned impressive tool. He states emphatic that the pores in the skin proves it's teetotal ancient. Also he says mebby the's an inscription. Other impressive fellers says it's a petrified body that walked the earth before history started up."

"Very well," I said. "I will start an action. But not an action based upon the assumption that this carving is either petrified flesh or of great antiquity. But upon the ground that it is the genuine Cardiff Giant and is entitled to that exclusive designation."

"Suits me to a *T*," Hannum declared. "What I want is fur the squabble to git into the newspapers."

I had scant hopes of succeeding in any action brought against Mr. Barnum, but Hannum had a right to his day in court; so, as soon as papers could be prepared, I filed suit. By this time, the third week in an exceptionally cold December, the giant was shipped from Albany to New York and placed on exhibition there. Barnum, always alert, immediately advertised that Hannum's giant was a fraud and that his giant was the genuine and original. Which, of course, whetted public interest and attracted large crowds of spectators.

Our two families—Lossie's and mine—always had made a great to-do over Christmas. One year the tree would be set up in our front parlor and the next year over at the Foxes'. Lossie and I always had gone with our fathers back into the hills to cut down the tree, and had made an occasion of it. And days before Christmas we busied ourselves stringing popcorn—it seemed like miles of it—with which to festoon the spruce boughs. And our presents, gaily wrapped, were stacked about the foot of the tree, ready to be distributed at dawn. Lossie and I were stirring before daylight, eagerly arousing our parents, who indulged us on this day as on no other day of the year.

This year, even though I had attained manhood and had opened my law office, and though Lossie had been upon her travels in Europe, there was no change in our preparations and little abatement in our excitement and enthusiasm—especially in Lossie's, who, as the day approached, seemed to shed years in the most remarkable way and to journey back into childhood. I admit that I was not far behind her, though I was somewhat ashamed of my eagerness and tried to assume a nonchalance and dignity which I was far from feeling.

Our families were dining together on the Sunday before Christmas when mother broke a silence, speaking to Mrs. Fox.

"I've been thinking," she said.

We all fell silent and waited, because when mother used that formula we knew that something was coming which we would either like very much or dislike heartily. It would be something unusual.

"You've been thinking?" said my father.

"That," said my mother, "Madam Janeway will be alone on Christmas Day."

There was a silence—almost an appalled silence. Then Lossie said breathlessly, "But it's our day. Our day!" She looked sideways at me for support. And not alone for support. There was something else in her eyes which I, always sensitive to her moods, understood. She was, for some reason, shocked at the idea of Madam Janeway sharing our Christmas festivities.

"There never," I said, "has been anyone besides our families."

"But," Lossie's mother said, siding with my mother, "we mustn't be selfish. It isn't as if you children were babies any more. You're grown up."

"Not on Christmas Day," Lossie said, quite loudly for her. "I won't be grown up on Christmas Day! I want it to be like always."

"Lossie," chided her mother, "don't be a silly child."

"But, auntie," I said, "Lossie's right. It's our day. There shouldn't be strangers—especially——" I stopped there, for I had been about to say "especially Madam Janeway." I heard Lossie suck in her breath. Somehow I felt that of all people in the world, Madam Janeway was the last we should include in our intimate merrymaking, but I could not say so nor explain why I felt that way.

Lossie was bobbing her head energetically in agreement.

Our parents did not know. They did not know, as we did, that there was something peculiar about Madam and about her relations with her servant, Oscar. In all Syracuse there was nobody besides Lossie and me who knew that all was not normal in that house across the street. What it was we did not know. But it was some unhappy thing, and we felt, instinctively perhaps, that the unhappy thing should not be permitted to intrude upon our happy intimacies. I thought miserably of that strange conversation we had overheard between Madam and her servant; I knew Lossie was thinking of that shocking scene we had witnessed through the window when Madam had smashed her mirror to flinders.

"I'm surprised at you children," said Auntie Fox, "when she's so good to you, and so generous to everybody."

And that was true. Madam had been good to Lossie and me—especially to me. She was my first important client. She was forever doing thoughtful little things for both of us, and would have overwhelmed us with generosity if we had been willing to accept. It was a fact that she had a heart that extended sympathy to everyone who needed sympathy, and a lavish hand to come to their aid. And she was so beautiful and so stately. It was not easy to think any evil of Madam. But nevertheless Lossie and I knew she was entangled in some sort of web of badness. And it was unendurable that that web should be permitted to touch our kindly, gentle, joyous yuletide.

"We'll discuss it in the parlor," Uncle Lander said,

pushing back his chair and rolling his napkin to shove into his napkin ring. So we all got up and traipsed into the parlor, where, before any discussion could get itself started, father and Uncle Lander would be snoozing in their rocking chairs. Lossie was facing the window, and I saw her lean forward and look out into the street.

"Madam's sleigh," she said. "But she's not in it. Oscar's on the seat beside the coachman." And then: "It's stopping here." It was, indeed, stopping before the house, and Oscar climbed down with something in his big hands. He mounted the steps to the front door and rang the bell. The hired girl came from the kitchen to answer the ring, and presently came into the parlor with two envelopes in her hand. She handed one to Auntie Fox and the other to mother, who received them with lifted brows.

"I declare!" mother exclaimed and opened her envelope. Now we in Syracuse did not go in much for engraved invitations, but this was an engraved invitation, very expensive and stylish. Mother read it and repeated herself, but with emphasis. "I do declare," she said.

"What," asked my father testily, "do you declare about?"

"It's an invitation from Madam Janeway for Christmas Eve," mother said, emphasizing again. "Dinner and entertainment. The idea! Christmas Eve!"

"Well," said Uncle Lander, "that takes the cake."

"A big party—a big, formal party on Christmas Eve," said Auntie Fox.

"But," expostulated mother, "people here just don't

have big parties on Christmas Eve. Any other night, but not that night."

"Maybe," suggested Auntie Fox, "folks do different in New York or wherever she comes from."

My mother was firm about it. "She should have made inquiries before she went ahead," she said severely. "Naturally, we shan't go."

"Hold your hosses, ma," father said. "Better wait to see how the rest of the town takes it. Me, I bet Mr. and Mrs. Banker Watts and their set'll be there with bells on."

"And the Proberts," said Uncle Lander. He clucked and closed his eyes. "Ma," he said, "I calc'late we'll be almighty conspicuous if we don't go. Hohum!" He yawned mightily. "Won't be many'll be able to resist those engraved invitations. Shouldn't be surprised if a new set of social doodads had come to Syracuse. . . . Mrs. Fox, mebby tomorrow you better go shoppin' for a butler."

Well, that closed the discussion about inviting Madam Janeway for Christmas, but it was far from abating the furor caused in town by Madam's invitation and the date chosen for her party. At the end of twenty-four hours the consensus was that Madam did not understand, being a newcomer, but that she meant well, and it would be a very ill way of repaying her for her many benefactions to snub her and absent ourselves from her party. Besides which, our curiosity was aroused and perhaps some emotions unworthier than curiosity. We took it for granted that the dinner would be something to talk about, and the entertainment to follow would be lavish, in accordance with Madam's wealth and custom.

Consequently, all who had been bidden and were not confined to bed by illness crowded into Madam Janeway's house on Christmas Eve of the year of 1869.

Our two families crossed James Street together, our mothers ahead, then our fathers in decorous black, and bringing up the rear were Lossie and I. Lossie was no hoyden tonight. Her hair, always lovely, was piled high upon her little head; her shoulders, until she covered them with her cloak, were bare, and lace gloves protected her hands and arms. Her walk was a stately progress as her fingers daintily grasped her hooped skirt and held it above her ankles as she picked her way across the street. She was remote and self-assured, and I did not know what to do about it. She condescended to me and was able by some black magic to make me feel younger than she, and gawky and altogether like a country bumpkin. I was furious with her for putting on such airs even before we got to the party, and I sulked. I felt her looking at me out of the corners of her eyes.

"Orrin Applegate," she said in a crisp voice, "if you would stop growing and stand up straight and hadn't such outrageous big feet——"

"I'm as God made me," I said sourly. "At least I'm not a vain little snip."

"Precious little you have to be vain about," she retorted.

"It may be nothing to be proud of," I said straitly, "but at least I'm not ashamed of my friends."

She laughed a cool, tinkling little laugh. "What a finely matched couple you and that gigantic Susie Crampton would make! With her sheep's eyes and her simper."

"While," I said sullenly, "you and I are not matched at all. I suppose you're thinking we are Beauty and the Beast."

"Why," she said, "even that might be." She laughed again, that artificial, tinkling laugh. "How did that fairy story come out, Orrin? I forget."

By this time we were mounting the steps, and the door was opened to us by Oscar, whose death's-head face certainly did not constitute a warm welcome. Almost immediately we were swallowed up in the press of guests and, as always seems to happen in any social gathering, Lossie was immediately separated from me and became the center of a group of drooling men, young and old —one of whom, I noted with disgust, was oily old Jethro Willis, the Binghamton banker who had come all this way from home to be Madam's guest.

Madam Janeway was almost regal. She stood like some queen dispensing favors, gracious, stately, but at the same time so humanly and warmly beautiful and desirable. Banker Watts stood as close to her as he could manage, with his onion eyes almost hanging out upon his cheeks. She waved a welcoming hand to Lossie across the room and the two lovely women smiled at each other with no discernible trace of jealousy, which was incredible, for in that room were two courts, one presided over by Madam, the other by Lossie. I knew little of women, but this did seem to me a state of affairs which would be intolerable to both of them.

The house had been rearranged for the party, with tables set to accommodate all the guests. It was whispered about that Madam had imported the cook, or chef, from a famous restaurant in New York, with his helpers. And belatedly making a dramatic entrance glittering with jewels, appeared the majestic figure of Lucilla Bardoni, an opera star newly imported from Italy, who was to sing for us after dinner.

We found our designated places, and I was a bit surprised to discover that Lossie was at my right. I doubted that she was pleased to have me as her dinner partner, but I resolved to do my best to conduct myself as a man of the world. It was such a feast as never had been served before in Syracuse. Half the dishes I did not recognize, and doubted that any other guest was familiar with them, and a different wine with each course made me a trifle giddy.

But the lavish thing about the dinner was the favor at each plate—to each guest a Christmas gift, rare and costly. This largess alone must have cost Madam Janeway thousands of dollars. And when you added to that the expense of the exotic food, of the imported chef and crew and the fee for the Italian opera singer, then the total cost of this entertainment was such as could be afforded only by some Indian nabob or by a Vanderbilt or Rothschild—or a Dan'l Drew.

Lossie gave me her shoulder for the most part and bestowed her charms upon an elderly gentleman who sat on her right. He, I learned upon making inquiry, was an officer of some bank down the Hudson River at Kingston. Her talk—such sentences as I could catch—was witty and sophisticated, and, to me, most displeasing. But I could not deny that she had a talent for it. She could, I said ruefully to myself, have held her own with the young Queen Victoria of England.

The Italian woman sang songs which doubtless were wonderful and very high class, but which I did not enjoy. This was after we had left the table. I was not enjoying myself, and made my way out of the crowded rooms, intending to be very adult myself and smoke a cigar in Madam's office. But the office was occupied. Madam was there, and I recognized the oleaginous voice of Banker Jethro Willis from Binghamton. I paused before intruding.

Willis was speaking. "I brought it myself, Madam Janeway," he said. "I would not trust it to the mails or to other hands. I—er—preferred to have it appear to you as a personal favor from me."

"How charming, Mr. Willis," said Madam sweetly.

"It's here. I've sealed it in this envelope. If you would care to count it."

"Indeed not!" Madam exclaimed. "That would imply a doubt of your integrity—which is unthinkable."

Willis purred like a great alley cat. "You will find it correct. A considerable sum." He cleared his throat. "One hundred thousand dollars in lawful currency of the United States."

"I'm sure I'm obliged to you, sir. You are indeed

most amiable."

I thought that a curious word to use in the circumstances. An odd and somehow inadequate expression of thanks for the loan of so great a sum as a hundred thousand dollars. I did not remain to listen further, but walked quietly away and rejoined the guests in the parlor.

When I opened my office door on the Monday morning after Christmas Day I experienced an odd feeling of discomfort, as if something were not right with the room. It was almost as if someone were hidden there and as if I were conscious of malignant eyes staring at me. But no one was there, for there was no place of concealment whatever.

I crossed to my desk and found nothing had been disturbed. But I was still not satisfied. I peered out of the window; I scrutinized the walls. It was not until I cast my eyes upon the floor that there was some confirmation that an intruder had been there.

Leading from the door to Madam Janeway's safe was a line of all but invisible spots of dampness, as if someone with wet shoes had walked there. I bent over the tracks, if tracks they were, and satisfied myself that someone to whose soles clung freshly fallen snow had walked from door to safe, had paused before the safe, and then had returned to the door and gone away.

I tried the safe's door and it was firmly locked. If it had been opened, it must have been by someone who possessed the combination. It was puzzling and disturbing. It seemed so purposeless for an intruder to effect an entrance to my office, to walk to an empty safe, pause there possibly to open it, and then to go away again.

I sat in my chair and stared at the iron strongbox. It seemed that I, whose life had been so comfortable and uneventful, had suddenly become afflicted with mysteries, and that the serenity I had always enjoyed had unaccountably been sullied by violence. Nothing ever had happened to me, from my birth until the arrival of Madam Janeway in town, that could not be cured by the application of arnica or court plaster or a bit of beefsteak on a blackened eye.

But now, without reason or warning, there had been close to me two murders by throttling and the acquisition of a wealthy and beautiful client who appeared to be unhappily in the power of an uncanny man who seemed to serve her as butler. And this butler Lossie and I had seen assiduously practicing his art of knife throwing in the barn. There had been, also, that resemblance between Madam and the chief man of the medicine show, Gideon Weeks, strangled probably by the same fingers that had wrung the neck of the Duke and, with macabre humor, set him upright in my father's carriage for us to find.

And as recently as Christmas Eve I had been a witness to the delivery to Madam Janeway of a hundred thousand dollars by the repulsive little banker from Binghamton. And reaching out like an invisible octopus from Madam's residence were unsubstantiated rumors connecting her with the miserly old millionaire, Dan'l

Drew. Rumors not so nebulous and unsubstantial to me, who had seen his signature on the outside of sealed packages of securities, or to Banker Watts or Banker Willis, or even to Banker Dewitt from Albany.

The uncomfortable thing—the most uncomfortable thing about it all—was that I and Lossie Fox were the only people in Syracuse who had seen things we were not meant to see, who had had our suspicions aroused that something of ill omen went on under the gay and opulent surface presented by Madam. And we, aware of hidden evil, had not the slightest inkling of what that evil might be or what appalling climax hung over our heads.

I sat striving to reason things out, but reached no firm conclusion. It is futile to reason without all the data, for one small, missing bit can make all ratiocination futile. One misreading of a thing by me that morning came uncomfortably close to being ruinous to myself and to bringing upon me, innocent as I was, a complete debacle. This small thing was that it never occurred to me that the purpose of an intruder in opening a locked safe might not be to abstract something from it, but surreptitiously to place something inside it.

No clients making their appearance, I passed away the time by memorizing the fourth section of the Statute of Frauds—about being responsible for the debt or default of another only when a written statement exists. Eleven o'clock arrived and through the window I could see snow falling in large flakes of the sort that told me there would be walks to clean that night.

I withdrew my eyes from the street when there

came a peremptory rapping on my door. I called permission to come in and Madam Janeway's butler, Oscar, clomped into my office, slapping snow from his hat and coat and kicking it from his enormous feet. There was something deliberately offensive in the way the man mussed up my floor and then stared at me as if challenging me to resent his conduct. As he stood across the desk from me, with an expression on his bony face that was close to a sneer, he reminded me of a huge bird of prey out of some medieval tale of horrors. He towered over me as I sat, though he was not taller than I when we both stood erect. There was extraordinary width to his shoulders, but otherwise he was a gaunt bag of bones that somehow suggested irresistible strength. I could not but wonder how we would come out if sometime events forced us to have a go at each other.

"Well?" I asked curtly.

"Get to Madam's house as fast as your legs will carry you," he said in his harsh, grating voice.

I stared up at him, but his eyes did not waver.

"Is that," I asked, "the message Madam bade you deliver to me?"

"It's the git of it," he said. I understood him to mean the gist of it.

"Suppose, then," I said, "you start again and deliver the message in Madam's words, not in your impudent version of them." I stood up and pushed my chair backward. Even though he came from Madam Janeway, I did not propose to tolerate discourtesy from him. He stared back at me and there was a cold blaze in his small pig eyes. Then his thin lips parted in a vulpine grin.

"Feeling your oats, eh, rooster?" he demanded.

"Deliver your message properly," said I, "or get the hell out of here!"

He hesitated, and then bowed mockingly from the waist. "Madam Janeway," he said mincingly, "bids me request that you call upon her at your earliest convenience about a matter of considerable importance."

I have seldom been more angry, for this creature was plainly bent upon belittling me.

"You will inform Madam," I said, "that I will be with her before noon. You might add that when next she sends a messenger to select one with more good manners than skill in throwing knives."

The instant I spoke I knew I had let my anger betray me into making a fool of myself. Silence ensued. We both stood motionless—I appalled at my betrayal of dangerous knowledge, he digesting what I had said and making up his mind what to do about it. To my astonishment, he decided to ignore it.

"I will repeat your answer to Madam, exactly," he said with a politeness of which I did not think him capable. He bowed with some dignity, turned on his heel and strode out of my office. He closed the door gently behind him. I would have felt better had he slammed it. I confess that his change of manner from impudence to gracious courtesy was a frightening thing, and I felt an icy hand press my back between my shoulder blades.

* * 12 * *

I PUT on overshoes, coat, tippet and cap, and sallied out into the storm. It was not an unpleasant storm. Snow fell thickly in great flakes which fluttered downward to increase the depth of the white blanket that covered the earth. All griminess and hideousness of form were hidden or softened, and the most out-rageous structures erected by man were made beautiful by this white magic. It came to me suddenly that I wished Lossie were there with me, wading gaily, laughing, en-joying the peaceful loveliness of it all.

I reached Madam's residence and trod a path up the walk and the unswept steps. It was Oscar who answered my ring, and he ushered me into the little office as if nothing lay between us except that which would naturally lie between servant and visitor.

Madam Janeway sat behind her flat mahogany desk with its inset top of handtooled leather. She smiled and waved me to a chair.

"You must overlook Oscar's manners," she said gently. "He is sometimes very clumsy. You handled the matter admirably. It has augmented my good opinion of you, Orrin."

I wondered if Oscar had related to her all that passed between us, including the matter of my remark about knife throwing. But I did not ask.

"Will it be possible for you," she asked, "to undertake a mission to Albany for me?"

"Leaving when, Madam?" I asked.

"On the first possible train," she said.

"In that case I shall have to hurry," I told her. "What do you wish me to do in Albany?"

"You will," she said, "call upon Mr. Horatio Dewitt at his bank and deliver into his hands a package I shall entrust to you, and take his receipt for it, and receive from him a sealed envelope in return."

"Is that all, Madam?"

"It seems like a mere errand," she said with an understanding smile, "and beneath the dignity of a member of the bar. But I assure you that is not so. It is of first importance." She hesitated and her eyes lost their sparkle as she gave thought to some matter that seemed to trouble her.

"Orrin," she said, "I rely upon your discretion."

"You may do so," I assured her.

"Mr. Dewitt is a most inquisitive person," she said. "He will ask troublesome questions. He is a prying man."

"I shall be very ignorant, Madam."

She raised her eyes to mine, and now they were bright and quick with intelligence and with a touch of malice.

"Not too ignorant, Orrin," she said. "Sometimes a

very smart young man can seem to be naïve."

I tried to read what was in her mind, but could not do so. Evidently she did not want me to be completely close mouthed with Mr. Dewitt, but what did she wish me to disclose and what did she wish me to retain?

"Upon what matters shall I be indiscreet?" I asked and smiled.

She returned my smile cozily. "If I should open yonder safe," she said, "it would be but natural for you to glance inside."

"Nothing," I replied, "could be more natural."

"Mr. Dewitt, knowing you to be my attorney, might bring up the matter of safes," she said. "He might even try to take you by surprise with a question."

"About this safe," I asked, "or the one in my office? To which, by the way, I have not received the combination."

"This safe, of course," she said a trifle sharply. "Why do you speak of the other one?"

"Because," said I, "it was visited early this morning."

"How do you know that?" she demanded.

"The intruder forgot to scrape his feet," I said. "Traces of footsteps remained."

"Did the safe seem to have been tampered with?"

"If it was opened," I replied, "it was by someone with the combination."

"Then you need not vex yourself," she assured me. "No one but me has that combination. But to return to Mr. Dewitt. If he asked a question about the contents of my safe, what would you reply?"

"That it seemed," I said, "to be full of documents and stocks and bonds."

"Seemed?" she asked with raised brows.

"That it was filled with documents and securities," I amended.

She nodded her head and then she lowered it and seemed to blush. "Orrin," she said, "you have heard rumors about me—odd rumors connecting my name with that of an eminent gentleman in New York."

"Everyone has heard rumors," I told her.

"What gentleman was named?" she pressed me.

"Dan'l Drew," I said flatly.

"I have been named his mistress," she said unhappily, "or his daughter."

"Yes," I answered.

"Mr. Dewitt might bring up the point," she said, "he being so inquisitive."

"He might, indeed," was all I could think of to say.

"I would prefer, as any decent woman would," she said, "to be his illegitimate daughter rather than his mistress."

"Naturally," said I, though it seemed to me that any decent woman would prefer to be neither. "If he questions me on the point, I could state that professional ethics estopped me from discussing it."

"But," she said, and stared at me fixedly, "as my trusted attorney you would be apt to know the truth?"

"I do not know the truth," I said firmly.

"But you do," she said, nodding her beautiful head

and smiling graciously, "know that I prefer to be gossiped about as his daughter."

"That I know, Madam," I said.

"Which," she said, "if taken by surprise, you might be betrayed into mentioning."

"I think, Madam," I said, not too pleased about the whole business, "that I have my instructions."

She arose and went to her small safe, which she opened deftly, kneeling so that I could see over her shoulder into the interior. From a pigeonhole she extracted a thick packet, sealed with red wax and made more secure by tape. This she handed to me. I placed it in my coat pocket.

"See to it," she said, "that you get a receipt in addition to a packet Mr. Dewitt will give you in return." She extended her hand with its long, tapering fingers and almond-shaped nails. "Good-by, Orrin. I'm so happy to have one upon whom I can rely."

I left the house. Oscar saw me to the door silently. I plowed my way across the street to my home, where luncheon was awaiting me, then I packed a small bag with things necessary to a trip to Albany. I walked briskly down to our new depot, which had been dedicated by Mr. Vanderbilt not long ago.

I was catechized by Mr. Dewitt in a manner that made me respect his abilities as a cross-examiner, but, in actuality, there were few definite answers I could give him. I am quite sure he thought I was evasive and, contradictorily enough, I became convinced that the less I told him the more I rose in his estimation.

"For so young a man," he said to me, "you can be most skillfully close-mouthed. It is a quality I admire. Generally when there is meat in a nut I am able to crack it. You serve Madam Janeway well. Should I or this bank ever have legal business in Syracuse, I shall bear you in mind, Mr. Applegate."

"I thank you, sir," I said, and was much set up by his compliment.

"To return to the subject of Dan'l Drew," he said persistently, "just what was it you said to me?"

"I said, sir, that if there was gossip about Madam, connecting her name with that of Mr. Drew, she would prefer to be called his illegitimate daughter rather than his mistress."

"Did you take that to indicate, Mr. Applegate, that she actually is the old rascal's daughter, born on the wrong side of the track?"

"I do not think," I replied, "that Madam Janeway ever was his mistress."

He grinned at me suggestively. "You prefer to think of her as sinned against rather than as sinning?" he asked, and chuckled moistly. He rose and went out into the banking room, returning presently with a sealed envelope of heavy paper, which he pushed across his desk to me. I had already, according to instructions, delivered to him Madam's packet of securities.

"You will sign this," he said, handing me a paper which I read carefully. It was a receipt for a hundred and twenty-five thousand dollars.

"Your pen, if you please," I said, and taking a fresh piece of paper wrote a receipt in language I preferred. Instead of acknowledging that I was taking this great sum in currency, I wrote cautiously that I acknowledged receipt of a sealed envelope purporting to contain this money.

Mr. Dewitt read it and again chuckled. "Self-preservation is the first law of nature," he said, and tore open the envelope. "Count it," he said shortly.

I did so. The sum was correct. "Now sign," he directed.

I did so, and in return asked his receipt for Madam's stocks and bonds. The package containing them lay at hand, listing on its outside its contents. His receipt had been prepared, listing the securities described. He tossed it across to me, but, to my surprise, did not open the package to make sure of its contents.

"Tell Madam Janeway," he said unctuously, "that I am delighted to be able to accommodate her—and Mr. Drew. A pleasant trip back to Syracuse, Mr. Applegate."

We struck hands and I walked to the railroad station, where I took a train home, feeling an uncomfortable sense of responsibility for the huge sum of money I carried in my inside pocket. On arrival, I took it at once to Madam's home, where I was admitted to her office.

"Madam," said Oscar in his harsh voice, "will be down in a minute."

On her desk, open as if she had been reading from it, was the big scrapbook which she had shown me on another occasion. I was able to read the headlines of an article pasted upon the page, though the printing was upside down to me.

"SENTENCED FOR FORGERY," it said. And its subheading was: "WOMAN GIVEN LIGHT SENTENCE FOR CLEVER CRIME AND IMPERSONATION."

More I could not make out, nor did I have a chance to turn the book so I could read the smaller type. Madam came in, smiling graciously.

"All went well?" she asked.

"There was no hitch," I said. "Here is the money."

"For which you gave a receipt?"

"After counting it," I said, preening myself on my caution.

She became suddenly very still, but then relaxed and made no comment. It was clear, however, that she was displeased that I had insisted upon making a count of the bills. I could not understand why. She opened her safe and put the money inside. She did not reseat herself, but held out her hand to me and thanked me for taking care of the matter for her.

"Hereafter, Orrin," she said, "your monthly retainer will be a hundred dollars."

This was pleasant hearing and I walked buoyantly across James Street to our front steps. Lossie's front door opened and she called to me, and when I reached her porch she said, "I've been watching for you. Come on in. There's popcorn and molasses taffy."

She was no princess now, but a little girl with sticky fingers, chewing almost greedily upon a mouthful of candy. "Help yourself," she said indistinctly when I was inside and my overcoat removed. And then: "I love to ride on trains. Do you love to ride on trains?"

"I don't count it an amusement," I said.

She licked her fingers and made a face at me. "My, my. Important man of business," she said.

"Well," I answered indiscreetly, for I had no objection to magnifying myself, "it was pretty important. I brought back more money than you've ever seen."

"Lucky you didn't lose it," she said. "What if there had been a train robbery?"

"But there wasn't," I said. "And Madam was so pleased she raised my monthly retainer to a hundred dollars."

"Tomorrow," she said, "you will buy me a present. But what were you all puckered up for when I saw you crossing the street? What worried you?"

"Why," I said, "for a moment Madam was displeased with me, and I couldn't figure out why."

"Tell," Lossie commanded.

"Well, she asked if I'd given Mr. Dewitt a receipt for the money. And I told her I had, but not until he had opened the envelope and allowed me to count it."

"Showing off," she said. "And she didn't like it?"

"She seemed not to," I said. "But she should have been pleased at my carefulness."

Lossie leaned forward and her eyes snapped as she peered at me like some saucy little bird. "And did Mr. Dewitt open his envelope?"

"No," I said.

"Perhaps," Lossie said, "Madam was mad because you set an example. Because you might have made him think it would be a good idea to do what you did and look inside the envelope."

"Nonsense," I exclaimed.

"I'll bet that was it," she said. "And I think Mr. Dewitt shouldn't be the head of a big bank. It'd be altogether too easy to pull the wool over his eyes."

"But this," I said, "was a transaction with Madam Janeway."

"Yes," Lossie said with a little grimace; "that's what Mr. Dewitt thought! All impressed by her and her grand airs and her extravagances and her beauty—and her nasty old Dan'l Drew. She just simply befuddles them."

"Why, Lossie," I exclaimed, "I thought you liked Madam Janeway. I thought you admired her. I thought you were such close friends."

She made an answer that I did not expect. It is a thing she often does. "Remember," she said, "how you and I took the kitchen clock apart?"

"Yes," I said testily. "You talked me into it, but it was I who got the razor strap for doing it, not you."

"Why did we do it?" she asked.

"I guess we wanted to find out what made it tick," I said.

Lossie was very serious. "From the first minute I saw her," she said, "I've wanted to know what makes Madam tick."

"Have you found out?" I jeered.

"Not yet," she answered, "but I've had a couple of peeks inside her case. There are lots and lots of wheels and sprockets and pinions. One of these fine days I'm going to find her mainspring."

"But," I repeated, "I thought you liked her."

"I do," she said. "Oh, I do like her. She's wonderful! She's lovable!" She pounded her knee with her little fist. "That's the trouble," she said. "Madam is just too perfectly marvelous to be true!"

I don't know that I ever have seen anybody eat popcorn and molasses taffy with the avidity of Lossie Fox. She stuffed herself with the greediness of a six-year-old.

"Good!" she exclaimed, working her jaws on a large, chewy bit. She tried to talk with her mouth full and I made out that she was asking, "Are you just simply abominably ethical, Orrin?"

"You'll have a stomach-ache," I warned; "and I'm ethical, if you mean professionally."

"I don't think I am," she said, swallowing. "I do not think women are strictly ethical. Not when they're all agitated with curiosity. It wasn't a woman that invented ethics. It was a rapscallion of a man. I'm going to ask you a question. Not a fact question, but a suppose question."

"A hypothetical question?" I said.

"Oh," she said, big-eyed, "aren't you just wonderful! Hypothetical! Here it is: Suppose somebody dropped something, and when they were gone you picked it up. And suppose it was a strange kind of a thing that made you break out in a rash of wanting to know what it was. Now, hypothetically, would you return it to the owner and simply strangle your curiosity or would you try to— to decipher it?"

"Decipher?"

"Yes"—she nodded vigorously—"like a puzzle."

"Why," I answered, "if I knew to whom it belonged, I would return it, of course, and not try to pry into something that didn't concern me."

"I was afraid you'd be like that, and not want to help."

"Help to solve this puzzle?"

"Yes. It's a dandy puzzle, and I made a copy of it, so I could return the original in a kind of sneaky way, so the person who lost it would never know I'd seen it."

"You are a devious, underhanded little snippet," I said.

"But, of course," she said, disregarding what I said, "you, being so ethical and upright and all, wouldn't want to even look at it."

"Why," said I—speciously I'm afraid—"if it would help you solve a moral problem, examining the thing could violate no obligation."

"That," she said, extracting a bit of taffy from a back tooth, "is a slippery answer. But before you go all noble and change your mind, here it is."

She handed me a visiting card, and the name on the card was Madam Janeway's. But that was not the matter of interest. What Lossie wanted me to see was on the back of the bit of cardboard. It was made up of lines and letters and figures like this:

O

R4 x 54

L3 x 73

R2 x 35

L

"How did you get this?" I asked.

"I drove Madam downtown to shop this morning in our sleigh, and she must have dropped it out of her reticule when she took out her handkerchief. I found it on the floor after she was gone."

Clearly the thing was some sort of memorandum, or cipher, or cryptogram. But there was something familiar about it. It reminded me of something—something to do with my father and Uncle Lander. I concentrated with might and main while Lossie chewed and watched me. And then I remembered. It had happened in their office, and Uncle Lander, who knelt in front of the safe, said ruefully, "I've forgotten the darn combination." And father said, "You always do, Lander. Here, I'll write it down for you once more, but, for goodness' sake, don't lose it again." So he scribbled on a card and handed it to me to give Uncle Lander. And it was made up of numbers and letters and *x*'s in much the same way as the one I now held in my hand.

"Lossie," I said, "I think I know what this is. Where's my hat and coat?"

"And where," she demanded, "do you think you're going?"

"To attend to something," I said evasively.

"If it has anything to do with this puzzle," she told me, "I'm going along."

"It's late," I objected.

"I'm grown up," she snapped. "It's not my bedtime yet. Where are you going, Orrin Applegate?"

"To my office," I said.

"Snooping?" she asked.

"Snooping," I told her hardily.

"What's become of your ethics?" she asked, and wrinkled her nose.

"If," I said, "this is what I think it is, it may even be that ethics requires me to look into it."

She ran for her coat and fur cap, and we went out of the house into the snow and plowed our way downtown. It was not a long walk, but we were puffing and blowing by the time we got to the building where my office was located. I let myself in and we climbed the stairs to my little cubicle. I made a light and, with Madam's card in my hand, I knelt before the safe the combination of which she had apparently neglected to supply me with. The safe that had been surreptitiously opened in the nighttime.

I put the knob at zero, and then followed the directions. Four times to the right to 54; three times to the left to 73; two times to the right to 35, and then a twirl to the left.

My deduction or memory or reasoning had been

correct. The figures had indeed been the combination to this safe, and I turned the handle and swung open the heavy door. Lossie squealed. I almost squealed myself. For there, in a safe supposed to be mine, in an office that definitely was mine, was stacked more money than I ever had seen in my life, carefully arranged in packets. I fingered them hastily and faced Lossie, who stared goggle-eyed.

"H-how much?" she asked breathlessly.

"About," I said, equally breathlessly, "a half a million dollars."

* * 13 * *

LOSSIE and I stared at each other blankly. Here was the reason someone had been entering my office in my absence—to put money in this safe! And here was the reason why Madam Janeway had not furnished me with the combination. Here in my office, in a safe, which everybody but Madam and me thought was my property, was secreted an enormous sum of money.

"I think," Lossie said faintly, "it would be a very stupid idea for me to return that card with the combination on it to Madam Janeway, to let her know that you or I had seen it."

"It could," I agreed, "be very unwise indeed."

"Why," she wanted to know, "would she hide all this in your safe instead of keeping it in her own?"

"Why should she keep it in anybody's safe?" I asked. "Why not deposit it in a bank?"

"Shut that safe door," Lossie said. "It frightens me to look at so much money."

I closed the door and twisted the knob. Lossie walked around the desk and took possession of my chair as if it were her right. She was curt and peremptory.

"Memorize the combination," she said firmly, "and destroy the cards."

My memory is excellent. I committed to it the letters and figures that made up the combination, and then tore the cards—the original and the copy Lossie had made of it—to small bits and put them in my coat pocket.

Lossie voiced a thought that had come to trouble me. "This," she said, perched like a precocious little girl in my big chair, "is a decidedly gimcrack, not to say grotesque, way for a client to treat her attorney!"

"So it seems to me," I agreed.

"Maybe," she said, looking very wise, "Madam has got 'attorney' mixed up with 'cat's-paw.' "

"How could I be a cat's-paw? What for?"

"Just for instance," Lossie asked, "what did you just do for Madam in Albany?"

I hesitated before answering, debating in my mind the propriety of disclosing a client's business to anyone. But the whole matter of my relations with Madam Janeway had arrived at a point where self-preservation demanded that I have some advice as to how to conduct myself. Maybe Lossie was not old enough or wise enough to be a suitable counselor, but she was smart as a steel trap and her advice might be better than some older person's.

"Why," I said, "I went to borrow some money for her."

"Madam is very rich. Why should she borrow money? Has she borrowed money from other people?"

"From Banker Watts and Banker Willis and others."

"Then, Orrin, maybe all this money in your safe has been borrowed."

"Possibly," I said.

"And hidden away in your safe. It is hidden."

"You could say so," I agreed.

"Even you are not supposed to know it is here."

"It is very puzzling," I said.

"It is very incredulous," Lossie said. "I mean incredible—I mean unaccountable—unless——"

"Unless what?"

"Unless something is going on that is just terribly artful and fishy and slippery. And maybe we had better stop being just agnostic about Madam Janeway and become downright atheist."

"Oscar," I said.

She brushed Oscar off for the moment. "Just let's suppose," she said, "that this money is like contraband and illicit and with a bar sinister on it. And if it comes to some kind of a pinch, Madam denies she knows anything about it. And it is found in your safe. What then, Mr. Orrin?"

"I do not like to think about it," I said dolefully.

"In all the city," Lossie said, "in all the state and maybe in all the nation, you and I are the only people who are agnostic about Madam and Oscar."

"With growing reason," I answered.

"It could be a slippery spot to stand on if it were discovered."

"I opened my big mouth to Oscar about knife

throwing," I admitted.

Lossie was pensive, not frightened, but thoughtful. "Orrin," she asked, "do you think those two murders had anything to do with this?" She flicked her hand at the safe.

"What reason have we to think so?"

"Medicine show," she said promptly. "The two men who were throttled were connected with the show. There was a knife thrower with the show. Things equal to the same thing are equal to each other. Hence Oscar was connected with the show. The first man was a snooper, and maybe he snooped too much in our neighborhood. The second man, Gideon Weeks, resembled Madam Janeway. Maybe he snooped."

"What you say is possible."

"And you and I have snooped," she said.

The conclusion to be drawn from that was obvious and needed no enlarging.

"When people get all nonplused," Lossie said, "they're apt to run around in circles. They're apt to get bewildered."

"That's possible," I told her, "but what bearing has that on our predicament?"

"It might be a dandy idea to nonplus Oscar and Madam. If they are noble and innocent parties, it can do no harm. If they're stealthy and sinful, it might help you and me."

"But, my child," I said patronizingly, "how could we nonplus them?"

She wrinkled her cunning nose at me, but beyond

that showed no resentment. "You're supposed to be the astute lawyer who thinks up capers and expedients," she said. "What if Oscar sneaked here to open the safe again, and the cupboard were bare?"

"What do you mean?"

"I mean wouldn't he be good and plenty nonplused?"

"You're leading up to something," I said.

"I'm leading up," she said, "to Oscar finding an empty safe and throwing a conniption fit."

"You," I said severely, "are trying to wangle me into taking that money out of the safe and hiding it somewhere else."

"Right the very first guess," she retorted.

"Oscar and Madam would know I had abstracted it."

"How?" she snapped.

That question had merit. How would they know it was I? I had not, they would be sure, the combination to open the safe. It might have the effect of arousing suspicion between themselves. Both had the combination. There had, as Lossie and I knew well, been friction between them. It might even cause each of them to suspect that the other had abstracted the money.

"And," Lossie said, following my thoughts as she so often did, "if it didn't cause trouble betwixt them, it would be life insurance."

"For whom?"

"For you and me," she said. "We would hold it as a hostage."

"A very reckless thing to do," I said firmly.

"*Toujours l'audace*," she quoted smartly.

"Which, translated," I said sullenly, "means always take a silly chance."

"Not a bit of it! They couldn't be sure you had abstracted it. If you did, they wouldn't dare harm you because nobody but you could tell them where you had hidden it."

"Unless," I said tartly, "they took a leaf out of the book of the Indians and drove splinters under my nails or built a bonfire on my stomach to induce me to tell."

She looked me over from pate to soles and turned up her nose. "Aren't you big enough," she asked, "to take care of yourself?"

"Why go looking for trouble?" I demanded.

"You don't have to," she said pertly; "you're in trouble up to your Adam's apple."

She knew how to be persuasive. Always she had talked me into doing things she wanted me to do. I hate to confess it, but Lossie Fox had always been able to twist me around her little finger. Besides, when I came to think it over, there was more common sense than peril in her idea.

"Suppose—just suppose—I was so foolish as to do what you suggest. Where would I hide all this money?"

"Oh, that!" she exclaimed offhandedly, as if it presented no problem. "Why, we'd take it to the safest place on earth, where it would be guarded by somebody as able to guard it as Ulysses S. Grant."

"And where would that be?" I demanded.

"Aboard Lizzie Ann," she said promptly, "under

the eye of Captain Zacharias Wheelright."

"You have it all planned out, haven't you?"

"I'm very quick at planning," she said. "When there is need for a plan, I go right to work to make one."

"When do we do all this?" I asked.

"Right off quick," she said. She was never one for postponing things.

"No," I vetoed.

"Why not?"

"Because," I said, "I think they will be putting a lot more money in this safe. They haven't put in the money I got from Albany yet."

Lossie was biting her thumb. "Yes," she said presently, "it will be better to wait. Until we have found out some more." She paused and bit her thumb some more. "Bankers are gullible," she said thoughtfully, "but then, everybody is gullible. The more fantastic a thing is the more eager folks are to believe it. Like the Cardiff Giant. Look at the famous people who have swallowed it without pepper and salt! And a fortune being made out of it. Nobody asks questions."

"What sort of questions would they ask?"

"The first one I would ask is where it came from," Lossie said. "Nobody bothers. And the same with Madam Janeway. Where did she come from?"

"Why, from New York," I said.

"How do you know?" Lossie asked.

"Why—why——"

"Exactly," Lossie said. "You took it for granted. She appeared out of nowhere and rented a big house and made a splurge and spent money like water. And all this Dan'l Drew business!"

"But," I objected, "she has money to spend, and she is generous with it. And she has stocks and bonds. And Dan'l Drew's signature."

"And," said Lossie, "Oscar throwing knives in the barn, and berating her not a bit like a servant when they are alone, and disappearing on the day of the barbecue, and smashing the mirror, as we saw her do. But mainly and principally hiding all this money in your safe!" She sat back in my big chair and shook her head furiously. "Gullible!" she said firmly.

"But," I said, "if we add up all we know, what does it amount to? What has Madam Janeway done that is wrong, or dishonest, or criminal? Suppose we shouted all we know from the housetops. What would it amount to? And maybe Banker Watts and Banker Willis and Banker Dewitt have investigated and not been gullible? What if they really know all about her?"

"Let's go home," Lossie said suddenly. "This office is cold. I can't think with cold toes. But I still say gullible."

Well, that was that. We went home and the half million dollars remained in my safe, at least for the time being, and life went on as usual. Mr. Hannum's lawsuit against P. T. Barnum came to trial and, as I had warned him, we were defeated. The judge held, as I had foreseen, that there was no cause of action in exhibiting an imitation of a humbug. But the trial had served its purpose. Papers all over the nation printed accounts of the case and crowds of the curious flocked to see both the original giant and Mr. Barnum's imitation of it.

After a while, business in New York began to fall off and the owners of our giant moved it to Boston, where it caused as much of a furor as it had done everywhere else. And Boston being the Athens of America and brimming with great minds and scientists and poets, there ensued a bigger argument about what it really was than had arisen any place else. The great pundit, Ralph Waldo Emerson, of whom everyone stood in awe, came to examine it and declared that it was astonishing. He said publicly that it was beyond even his comprehension, but that without doubt it was a bona-fide petrified human being. In consequence of this high pronouncement, the crowds paying admission to see the marvel doubled and trebled.

But the famous Dr. Oliver Wendell Holmes, who wrote the poem about the wonderful one-hoss shay and was celebrated as an anatomist, approached the matter with scientific skepticism. Somehow or other, he managed to bore a hole in the giant's head just behind the left ear and demonstrated that the interior of the skull was solid stone, with no indication whatever of there ever having been a brain. But he did join with those who held that the giant was a piece of sculpture of great antiquity. This caused a lull in business and the reduction of admission from a dollar to fifty cents. At this bargain price, several hundred men and women and children came to see and to wonder every day.

The winter continued to be one of the coldest even

the senior citizens of Syracuse could remember. Snow fell and drifted and was cleared off sidewalks until it was piled high in great ramparts along both sides of the streets. The canal was solid ice, so that it seemed the imprisoned boats never would be able to move again. What salt our fathers shipped had to be conveyed by train. Business was feeling the effects of the panic and there was hardship, though not so severe as in the bigger cities of New York and Philadelphia and Boston, where banks seemed to topple every day.

Almost alone of all the people in our little city, Madam Janeway seemed untouched by the money shortage. There was no abatement in her regal entertaining or in her charities or in her generosity to the young friends she cultivated and loved to have about her.

With all her lavishness there was no shrinking in the amount of money hidden in my safe, but, on the other hand, a startling increase in its total. I kept track of it day by day and totaled it at least once a week. Before we even thought of the coming of spring the total reached the enormous sum of eight hundred thousand dollars, and I, even in the favored position of Madam's attorney, could not tell where it all came from. I was able to surmise, but surmise only, that some of it, at least, was the proceeds of increased borrowings from old banks and new lending by new banks.

Again and again, Lossie and I tried to reach a solution of this mystery by reasoning, but we were not able to do so.

"Why," I asked again and again, "should a woman

who owns stocks and bonds amounting to millions, as Madam seems to do, be borrowing and hiding away such incredible sums of money?"

"And why, when old Dan'l Drew keeps on sending her more securities, should she borrow at all? Why, a king could live on the dividends that must pour in!"

"If only Madam Janeway were involved," I said, "I might not be alarmed or suspicious, because a woman, or so I understand, is prone to be eccentric in money matters."

Lossie snapped at me. "Women," she said, "are a heap sight smarter than men in money matters or any other matters. Orrin Applegate, I've got as many brains as you have, and I can use them a great deal quicker. You —you're stodgy!" she added.

"All right," I said; "if you've got so many brains and they work so smartly, let's see you use them now."

"That I'll do," she retorted. "If people borrow money, they have to pay it back. What happens when these banks demand payment of Madam's loans?"

"Why," I said, "she has plenty of money to pay."

"Stupid!" she exclaimed. "If Madam means to use the money in your safe to pay back loans, why did she borrow it at all, and not use it? And why does she hide it away? It's silly to think she would borrow all that money and hoard it just to pay it back when her notes fell due!"

"Then," I said, "suppose you tell me why she does it?"

"Well," she said, "one reason is to skedaddle with it

and leave all these banks holding the bag."

"But that doesn't make sense. Not with all the wealth she's had from Dan'l Drew and all he keeps on sending her."

"That," she said, "is the part that makes it so hard to figure out." Then she stopped and stared at me, big-eyed. "What," she demanded in a startled whisper, "if all that is make-believe?"

"That's just silly," I said.

"And what," she went on, paying no attention to me, "if it's all a gigantic fraud and confidence game? And the pair of them, when they've borrowed all they can, just disappear?"

The very thought appalled me. It was impossible, but I could not help envisioning the results of such a thing, especially in this day of financial stringency. The results would be too tragic to consider. Madam would leave behind her a dreadful mess of bankrupt banks and beggared depositors.

"Orrin," Lossie said, and one would not believe that so dainty a girl could be so grim and determined, "it's time we stuck in our thumb and pulled out the plum. High time."

"Yes," I agreed, "we must make it impossible for that hoard to vanish. Whether we're right or wrong, we simply must. Tonight I'll carry that money to the Lizzie Ann!"

"We will," corrected Lossie.

"No," I objected, knowing it was useless to protest.

"We're having a boiled dinner tonight," she said,

"and you love corned beef and cabbage and all. You come and eat with us. Right after, we'll take a carpetbag and——"

There would be no way of getting rid of her, so I surrendered.

"Lossie," I said dubiously, "what if we're crying wolf and there isn't any wolf?"

"How much more horrible," she said gravely, "if we left the money there and there was a wolf! That, Orrin, we don't dare risk."

"No," I said, frightened at the possibilities, "that we don't dare risk. But, Lossie, think of the responsibility we—I assume!"

"If," she said tartly, "there's a kind of a man I despise, it is one who hasn't backbone enough——"

I didn't let her finish. "Oh, all right! All right!" I said. "It's all right for you to enjoy the excitement of it, but I'm the one who goes to the penitentiary."

She wrinkled her nose at me. "I'll come often and peek through the bars at you," she said.

After eating enormously of a New England boiled dinner—and it is a marvel how much Lossie can stow away for so dainty a person—we put on outer garments to keep us comfortable against the cold and started out for my office. We thought it wiser to go by a roundabout way though there was little danger of being seen. Even if we had been seen, nobody would have given it a thought. But when you are bent on a mischief you have an absurd apprehension that the whole world is waiting

to pounce upon you. As the preacher says, "The wicked
flee when no man pursueth."

With caution, we entered the building where my
office was and climbed the dark stairs. I fumbled for the
keyhole and got the door open, and we entered like
burglars. By the light of a single match, which Lossie
held for me, I opened the safe and scooped its contents
into a large carpetbag which I had concealed under my
overcoat. We were breathless.

I closed the safe door and twiddled the knob, and
there we were in the darkness, Lossie and I, with nearly
a million dollars on our hands.

"We are doing the right thing," Lossie whispered
to reassure herself.

"If I didn't think so," I whispered back sharply, "I
wouldn't be doing it. But right now I can feel Oscar's
fingers throttling me."

Now I don't know why I said that or what put the
thought into my mind, but as I crouched there in the
dark, it came to me that Oscar had a strangler's hands,
and that the gaunt man with the death's head was the one
who had already killed two men for reasons best known
to himself. I wondered why he had used his fingers instead of throwing a knife.

One thinks of a million dollars as a vast sum, but it
was surprising to me how small was the bulk of it and
how light the weight. I stood erect and shuffled to the
door with Lossie's hand on my arm. Outside, I set the
bag down on the floor while I locked the door behind
us. Then we slunk down the stairs and, hesitating in the

entrance, peered fearfully up and down the street. It was deserted, and Lossie and I were thankful for the icy breeze and the driving snow that kept folks within doors.

So heavy was the snow that one could not have recognized a friend six feet away, and it gave us a feeling of safety which was most welcome. Ten minutes buffeting the storm brought us to the basin and the spot where Lizzie Ann was tied. Smoke rose from the chimney and a welcome light gleamed below. We did not shout, as we usually did, but clambered aboard and rapped on the door.

"Who's there?" demanded Zacharias Wheelright.

"Lossie and Orrin!" I called back.

The door was jerked open and warm air fragrant with the aroma of fresh-baked bread welcomed us.

"And what," demanded Captain Wheelright, "be you younkers doin' abroad on sich a night?"

"It don't matter a mite," said Zach's woman, "what fetches 'em. They're welcome as posies in May."

She kissed Lossie, calling her "Lizzie Ann," as was her custom, and we seated ourselves near the roaring stove. Zach, seeming more gigantic than he actually was in those cramped quarters, peered at us with big, mild blue eyes while his woman bustled about like a hen with chickens.

"Still yourself, woman," he said. "Hush your fuss. Somethin' fetches the younkers here that hain't merely jest a sociable visit."

"We're bringing you trouble," Lossie said.

"Ye fetched it to the right market," said Maw

Wheelright promptly. "Troubles we've learnt to endure, be they ourn or another's."

"We've no right," I said.

"You that in a measure come to replace her we lost," said Maw Wheelright gently, "hain't got no call to speak of havin' a right. . . . Have they, paw?"

"Nary," said the big man gravely. "Has your trouble to do with that there carpetbag?"

"Yes," said I. "We've come to entrust it to you, Cap'n Zach. It holds close onto a million dollars."

"I swan to man!" the big man exclaimed. "That's a heap of cash, Orrin. Haow'd ye come by it?"

"Haow he come by it," interrupted Maw Wheelright, flitting like a wren on its perch, "hain't no concern of ourn. All we need know is what the lad craves us to do with it."

"It's a long and puzzling story," I said to them, "and maybe we've done a bad and foolish thing."

"Foolish mebby," snapped Maw Wheelright, "but not bad."

Zach blinked his great blue eyes and lighted his pipe and puffed slowly for a minute.

"Has this here howdy-do got suthin to do with that there fancy woman?" he asked gently.

Now "fancy woman" was a term I would not have applied to Madam Janeway, so aristocratic and dignified and beautiful, but I did not quarrel with Zach's use of the word.

"It has to do with Madam Janeway," I replied.

"The woman and me has argued over her," Zach

said. "We come to conclusions."

This was a surprise to me. How this pair, secluded on their barge, had even heard of Madam Janeway I could not comprehend. Not until I thought it over. And then I remembered that canawlers know everything. They live apart, they are a people to themselves, and so, in a sense, are spectators.

"What conclusions did you come to?" I asked.

"We got our minds made up," said Maw Wheelright, "that she's a Jezebel in sheep's clothin'. And that man of hern comes fresh smokin' from the Pit."

This was direct and succinct enough to suit anybody, but what made me pause was Maw Wheelright's phrase "that man of hern." Women of Maw Wheelright's class did not in such connection use the word "man" to denote a male. Used as she used it, the word "man" meant husband or at least one who occupied the place of a husband.

"Oh," I exclaimed, shocked at this idea more than at the thought of Madam's being engaged in something criminal, "but that's impossible!"

"Because," Maw said in her nasal voice, "she fair to see and mannered, and he's ill-favored and ugly!" She smiled gently. "Age hain't yit give ye wisdom," she said. "Ye'll come to learn that the's a sort of woman that's drawed to what's evil of body 'n' soul, 'n' is as horrid to look at as she's sightly." She nodded briskly and, all of a sudden I knew what she meant, because I had read a story just published, by a Frenchman named Victor Hugo, who wrote about a creature whose face had been cut into a horrid grin and whose name was Gwynplaine, the clown.

"I calc'late," Zach said in his placid way, "we better git back to the cash money. How came ye by it, Orrin?"

I told him about my safe. How it had been a sort of gift to me by Madam, but how she always avoided giving me the combination. And I explained about my nocturnal intruder and how Lossie had come by the card with the combination written on it. And how we had opened the safe and found much money in it, which was added to, week by week, until it amounted to the sum at our feet in the carpetbag.

"So," Maw Wheelright said, "it was her put it there."

"More likely," Zach corrected, "that skeleton feller." He knocked out his pipe while Maw watched him alertly to see that he spilled no ashes on the floor. "But who did they steal it off'n?" he demanded.

"She—they didn't steal it," I told them. "It was borrowed from banks."

"I still say 'stole,'" insisted Zach, "no matter haow it was contrived."

Maw Wheelright peered down at the carpetbag at my feet with a wry expression. "You children have fetched us trouble," she said, not angrily, but merely as one who states a fact and accepts it. "It comes to me that the's a sight of woe packed into that carpetbag." She closed her eyes and her thin face became stark and uncanny.

"Hist," said Zach, "the woman gits fits of second

sight. One's come over her naow."

I felt something very like superstitious awe, and, looking at Lossie, I knew she was experiencing the same thing. When Maw Wheelright spoke again, it was not with her own cackling voice, but in deeper tones, unbelievably masculine and unchancy.

"Two has been murdered because of this here," she said. "And death's ahanging like a millstone over the heads of all that tampered with it this night." She paused and seemed to choke for breath. Zach Wheelright sat rigid, his huge hands gripped into fists. He motioned us to silence. "Half good and half bad," the little woman said presently. "That's the burden she's got to bear. A body can endure bein' teetotal bad, but to have the good half accusin' her day and night is a dreadful thing. Cruel she hain't," Maw said, as one who renders a judgment, "nor with the will to slay. Clever to plot 'n' plan 'n' trick, but killin's growed out of her trickery, and more's to come. And her forced to know it 'n' condone it! Pore critter! And one that's dead her own kith 'n' kin."

Again there was gurgling in her throat and difficulty of speech. But her voice returned, strong and commanding. "Zacharias Wheelright, my man, ye got a bounden duty. Ye got to stand a shield 'n' buckler betwixt them we love 'n' the wickedness that hovers over 'em."

Her body went limp and I stretched out an arm lest she fall from her chair. But she did not fall, and in an instant she opened her eyes and peered about her vaguely.

"Seems like I been fur off," she said in a whisper.

"One of your spells, Maw," said Zach.

"A talkin' spell?" she asked.

"In a voice that wan't yourn," Zach told her.

"I feel the need of a cup of tea," she said, stirring to her little feet. "Was what I said to be understood? Can it be put to use?"

"We understood, Maw Wheelright," Lossie said gently, "and it can be put to good use."

"My grandame was gifted too," Maw said, and put the teapot on to boil. "I mind it scared me the first time I seen it. We was ploddin' through strange and wild country, aridin' to new lands in a covered wagon. And a dry thirst come over me. Bein' a leetle one, I cried. And grandame woke up from a sleep and says in a queer voice, 'Hush your noise, grandchild. A quarter of a mile ahead, we swing to the right in a dell with hick'ry trees agrowin'. And there'll be found a livin' spring to quench your thirst.' " Maw Wheelright bobbed her head pertly. "And so it was, and we come onto the dell and the hick'ry trees and the livin' spring. The wonder was that grandame never passed that way before or heard the spot described to her."

The wind tore at Lizzie Ann as if to wrench her from her place in the basin, and the teapot sang on the stove. Maw Wheelright hummed as she set out cups and saucers and pungent ginger cookies.

"The childern," she said to Zach, "ought to be safe in their warm beds. You will see 'em to their door, my man, and let no harm come nigh 'em."

Lossie dunked her cookie and said to Maw, "Would you rather we took the bag of money away?"

"It's best left here," she said. "When you go I'll hide it sure 'n' safe. . . . Good night, my darlin' Lizzie Ann, and may lovin' angels sit to the four corners of your bed."

So, leaving the dangerous money where it stood, we went out into the night, and Zach could not be persuaded that we would be safe without him to guard us. And so we reached home, and no eye, either friendly or of an enemy, watched our coming and going under the cover of the storm.

We had done what we set out to do, wisely or unwisely. And what, in the end, we should do with the cache of money, we did not know. Nor did we know what action Oscar and Madam would undertake if and when they found it to be missing.

Zach bade us good night, and then stayed as if reluctant to go without some other word.

"Some," he said, "makes claim that second sight comes from the Evil One. Me, I maintain that depends on who's gifted with it. My woman's a good woman. Whatever's in her or comes out of her hain't evil, but comes from God."

With that, he turned abruptly on his heel and disappeared into the bluster of the storm.

** 14 **

I REACHED a determination, and that without assistance from Lossie. Indeed I did not tell her what I had made up my mind to do. But there seemed to me to be no other course I could follow and maintain my self-respect. I would have to inform Madam Janeway that I could no longer represent her as her attorney. This was a difficult thing to do, not because she was my principal client, but because I would be unable to give her any cogent reason for my action. I could not face her and tell her I believed her to be guilty of fraud or of some skillful plotting to obtain money. For I had no evidence to support me. If there was chicanery, I could not specify the manner of it. So far as I knew, each of her considerable loans in various banks was amply secured by collateral. Nowhere except in my mind and in Lossie's was there a shadow of suspicion of Madam.

She continued to dominate our social life. Everyone liked her, no party was a success without her presence, and to be omitted from her list of guests when she entertained was a minor calamity. Her benefactions continued and her lavish generosity to her friends persisted.

And always when she appeared in public she was serene, gracious, stately and beautiful. So how was I to inform her that my conscience would no longer permit me to act as her man of law?

A note from Madam came across the street for me while I was eating my breakfast. It requested me to call upon her before I went downtown to my office. Although I was reluctant to face her and make known my determination, I crossed the street and rang the front-door bell. I had been striving to formulate in my mind the phrasing of my resignation, but words would not come. Oscar opened the door and I stepped past him into the vestibule with not a coherent idea in my head.

Always I had felt that Oscar did not like me; but then, he seemed to like no one. This morning his reception of me was almost impudent and his skeleton face wore an expression which might have been a sneer. Then, with elaborate punctilio which was in itself ironic and impertinent, he said, "Madam awaits you in her office." He led the way to the little room where she attended to her business affairs and where the safe was into whose interior I had looked. It had been bulging with what I took to be securities.

Madam, sitting behind her desk, smiled up at me in the most intimate and friendly way, and bade me good morning and asked me to seat myself.

"Maybe, Orrin," she said, "it's an impertinence to ask you to call on this matter—which is not legal at all. But I'm a most inquisitive woman."

I stared across the desk at her, so lovely, so charming,

so aristocratic, and my resolution ebbed away. It was absurd to think for an instant that this beautiful woman could have any connection, however remote, with crime. One would as soon have accused the young and lovely Queen Victoria on her throne in England.

"This long winter," she said, "I have amused myself. To pass away the time, I've been prying into this Cardiff Giant. Of course, in spite of Mr. Emerson or Doctor Holmes or all the scientists and preachers in the world, it is a hoax."

"Yes, Madam," I agreed.

"But a clever hoax, and amazingly successful. And I itched to know how it was perpetrated. It was easy enough to find out that Stubby Newell was only a cat's-paw, and that the man behind the deception was that atheist cigar manufacturer in Binghamton."

"George Hull," I said.

"A saturnine and ironic man," she said. "Now, I discovered that Mr. Hull had something huge and heavy shipped to him from Chicago. Weighty machinery to manufacture cigars, he claimed. But through a banking friend in his town I was able to determine that not a piece of new machinery has been added to his factory for years."

"Yes, Madam," I said, not pleased with myself.

"I want you, Orrin, to trace that heavy shipment back to Chicago for me. It should be easy to do." She smiled gaily at me. "Naturally, I shall pay for your services. Call it a whim. But I'm amply able to pay for having my whims indulged."

"But, Madam——" I commenced.

"It will be such fun to expose the hoax and make fools of the solemn asses who have pronounced it genuine."

I could find no diplomatic way to tell her what I had come to say. I tried to blurt it out baldly, but sitting there and looking across the desk into her intelligent, well-bred face, I could not make myself say the words.

On that morning I was young, inexperienced. How was I to perceive that the most efficient quality a scheming woman, a woman engaged in the execution of a huge fraud, could possess was exactly that combination of assets which made up Madam's personality.

"It will be amusing," Madam said, with a light laugh, "to expose the—the hocus-pocus. Just for our own entertainment."

"Very well, Madam," I answered, and then she stood up graciously and extended her slender hand and bade me good morning. I went out still Madam's attorney, my ethics put to rout and my virtuous intention brought to nothing.

When I reached my office, there stood outside my door the figure of a man so muffled in a heavy coat, tippet, earmuffs and felt boots that I did not at once recognize him. It was not until he removed his cloth cap that I saw my visitor was Jethro Willis, the banker from Binghamton.

"Good morning to you, Mr. Applegate," he said, more politely than he ever had conducted himself toward me before.

"You are up and about early, Mr. Willis," I answered, unlocking my door and standing aside to admit the man to my cold office. He breathed steam in my face and his fish eyes were sly and worried. In my life I have encountered men I disliked, men I feared, men I distrusted, but of all the regrettable characters I have known, I think this man was the most despicable.

"How may I serve you?" I asked, hoping I would be unable to serve him at all.

He unwound himself from his scarf, but retained his mittens as he sat down in the chair at the right of my desk.

"I hear tell," he said, "that you're a mighty smart young lawyer."

To this compliment I made no response, but waited.

"Off and on," he continued, "a sight of things come up here that need lookin' after."

I continued to wait.

"Bein's you're jest startin' out, I figgered ye might be some cheaper'n what an older feller would be."

"If," I said, "you are looking for cheapness rather than ability, I suggest that you go elsewhere."

"Naow, naow, Mr. Applegate. Don't git het up. I'm a businessman."

"Very well," I rejoined; "then come to business."

There was, it was evident, something on his devious mind, but he shied away from coming out with it. I did not help him. He wriggled in his seat and his eyes shifted from one side of my floor to the other, and he spat a stream of tobacco juice into my cuspidor.

"I hear tell," he said finally, "ye got some rich— continental-rich clients."

This being none of his confounded business, I made no response. He mumbled to himself and then took the plunge. "One of these clients bein' Madam Janeway," he said, looking up at me out of the corners of his pale eyes. "Yeah. It's related to me she regards you high and sets store by ye."

"Suppose you come to the point, Mr. Willis," I said sharply.

"You're a big and handsome and sightly feller," said Willis. "Folks says she sets more'n jest legal store by ye. It's said ye got a way of influencin' her to do what ye want easy as fallin' off a log."

For an instant I did not follow him or grasp his despicable meaning, and then I pushed back my chair and strode around the desk and fastened my fingers in his collar to hoist him to his feet. I propelled him toward the door. He choked and clawed at my hand, and, as I opened the door to eject him, he became articulate.

"Ye better listen!" he said venomously. "Ye better give heed to me! The' could be big money in it fur ye, and ye might be able to fend off bad trouble fur your client and fur other folks."

I let him go. A mean, slinking, slandering creature such as he was might be dangerous. And if I listened to him and let his poisoned tongue wag, I might learn something I should know.

"Keep a decent tongue in your head," I said, "and I'll listen to you."

"Madam Janeway's borrowed money from my bank," he said. "It's my bank. I own it. I built it up."

"By foreclosing mortages," I interrupted.

"When folks owe me money, I calc'late to git it back," he said viciously. "Bein' her lawyer, ye know haow much Madam's borrowed off of me."

I neither admitted nor denied.

"It's a hundred thousand dollars," he said. "Equal to the capital of my bank."

"You were pretty eager to lend it," I said. "You fawned on her like a hungry puppy. You've got your security."

"Yeah. That I got, and Dan'l Drew's name on her notes. But it's made me dangerous short of cash. And she don't make no payments on account. Money's terrible hard to git jest to carry on business. And if anything was to happen—if fur some reason she didn't pay up, I'd be bankrupt."

"Why come to me? Why not go to her?"

"A feller like me don't want to give offense to Dan'l Drew nor to his—his lady—his left-hand daughter or whatever she is."

"But," I said, "you've got your security."

He looked at me like a weasel blinking out of its burrow. "Mebby I have. Mebby I hain't," he said.

"Meaning what?" I demanded.

"I got an envelope," he said, "all wound round with tape 'n' sealed tight with sealin' wax. And listed outside is the stocks and bonds that's inside. And Dan'l Drew's name's there. But I hain't never seen 'em with my own

eyes. What I wake up in the night 'n' ask myself is:
What if they hain't there? What if the's skulduggery?"

"Well," I said impatiently, "why don't you open
the package and see?"

"I dassen't," he said. "I dassen't make no enemy of
Dan'l Drew or his woman."

"Then what," I asked, "do you purpose?"

"I kind of contrived to come see you," he said in a
sort of whimper. "To see if I couldn't git you to make her
pay me back maybe at least twenty-five or fifty thousand.
That would keep me agoin'." He turned his head slowly,
and I was reminded of a saurian as he blinked at me.
"Oh, not fur nothin'. I calc'late to pay ye well. Say five
per cent of what ye kin git out of her."

"I'm not for sale that cheap," I said.

"I'll go ten per cent," he said eagerly.

"Mr. Willis," I said, "I want no truck with you
whatever."

He glared at me like a cornered rat. "Ye won't help
me none?"

"None," I said.

"Then mebby," he said, "you 'n' her'll regret it to
the last days of your lives. I'm capable of makin' mischief,
I be, and willin' to do so."

I strode past him and jerked the door open. A man
stood there in the hallway, and his position indicated
that his ear had been pressed against the panel of my
door. He straightened with a jerk and presented the
gaunt face and hollowed eyes of Oscar, Madam Janeway's butler. He stood aside for Jethro Willis to pass,

and then turned and looked after him until he disappeared down the stairway. There was something still and secret and frightening about the bony man whose shoulders were almost as wide as mine. His big hands with long, splayed fingers flexed, closing and unclosing, as his ophidian eyes burned into mine.

"What," I demanded, "are you doing here?"

"A message from Madam Janeway," he said. "A matter she forgot this morning."

He held out to me a sealed, perfumed envelope.

"Were you also," I asked, "required to apply your ear to my door?"

This did not abash him. He only widened his eyes, and his gash of a mouth parted in what I took to be his version of a grin.

"There was no need," he said. "Your voices were loud."

With that, he turned on his heel and walked away, and there was nothing I could say or do. Though I was certain he had followed me from Madam's house to spy, probably with knowledge that Jethro Willis was in town. And that his spying was with the knowledge, and perhaps with the consent of Madam, the note in my hand attested.

I closed the door and tore open the dainty envelope. The message it contained was of no importance. It merely informed me of incidental details of the carting of George Hull's crate of machinery from the city of Chicago eastward and of the breaking down of the wagon that carried it.

Perhaps my obligation as Madam's attorney was to acquaint her with what had passed between Jethro Willis and me. But I was sure it was information she would have from Oscar. I sat at my desk and stared out of my window at the day, now clear and still and icy, and pondered the implications and possibilities of Willis' predicament and terror and threats. Here was danger to Madam from an unexpected source; menace from the frightened jackal which might well bring down her house of cards. If, indeed, it was a house of cards. At any rate it was beyond doubt that her affairs had reached a climax. If she was above reproach she would satisfy Willis' demands by paying her debt to him. If, on the contrary, she was engaged in a monstrous chicanery, then some other sensational conduct would ensue. But what it would be I could not foresee.

When I went home to my midday meal I looked across the street to Madam's mansion. There were no signs of life. Its windows were blank and expressionless. One might almost have guessed it to be vacant. But then, as I mounted our steps, I looked again over my shoulder and could see into Madam's room. She was visible. She seemed to be ransacking her closet, for gowns and other articles of apparel were piled upon her bed beside two large pieces of baggage. Madam was preparing for a journey.

The rest of my day was vexatious and monotonous. No clients came to my office. I could not apply myself. I merely sat and worried, and as I did so I was aware of increasing tension, of a sense of some dire thing impending. It was as if I watched some great, menacing tempest approach and could do nothing but wait for the storm to burst.

I had slight appetite for supper. I could not even bring myself to cross our yards to Lossie's house and share my fears with her. I thought I would be unable to sleep, but I did drop off and slept fitfully, to awaken at an unpleasantly early hour. Restlessly I waited for breakfast time, and then walked reluctantly to my office. I unlocked and opened my door, and then stopped dead still just over the threshold. The shock I sustained had almost a physical impact. For the massive door of my safe stood open, exposing its empty interior!

During the night, an intruder—there was no doubt in my mind that it was Oscar—had invaded my office and opened the safe with the intention either to deposit more cash in it or to remove the sum approaching a million dollars that had been secreted there. And discovered that it had vanished.

I heard heavy feet pounding the floor of the hallway and my door was kicked open violently. Oscar stood there, bending forward from the waist and flexing his strong fingers. He was like some great, starved ape. I sprang to my feet. "Where is it?" he demanded and took a step toward me.

* * 15 * *

OSCAR stood midway between my desk and the door. At his right, against the wall, was the safe with its open door and bare interior. His arms were extraordinarily long and the hands that hung from bony wrists were larger than a man's hands should be, with fingers tense and bent like talons. It was clear to me that he had trespassed upon my office the night before, either to add to the hoard in the safe or to take from it. And now here he was to demand of me why he had found it empty.

"Where is it?" he asked a second time, taking another step toward me.

"Where," I countered, "is what?"

"Don't dilly-dally," he said. "The safe is open and its contents gone."

"Why ask me?" I demanded.

"Because," he replied, "nobody could have rifled it but you."

"Rifled it of what?" I asked, wasting time and postponing the moment of action. "And tell me," I said in my most determined voice, "how I opened the door?

Madam Janeway never gave me the combination."

"There is no lock that can't be opened," he said. "You opened this one. What did you do with the money?"

"If there was money in my safe, how did it get there?" I asked.

"Don't hoggle-boggle with me," Oscar said harshly. "Where is that money? Tell me before I choke it out of you!"

I had to put on a bold front; mainly, I suppose, to hold fast to my self-respect. I sneered at him. "Haven't you done enough throttling?" I asked. "Your score is two. It would be dangerous to make it three."

His wide slash of a mouth became a lipless line, but he did not take another step toward me. His pale eyes scrutinized me, estimating me, calculating the wisdom of an attack. I maneuvered for more time.

"Suppose," I said, "you succeeded in choking me to death. How would you gain? If, as you seem to think, I took something from this safe, I must have put it somewhere. A dead man can't disclose where he has cached a treasure."

He flexed his fingers. "You would talk," he said, almost in a whisper.

"Madam Janeway," I said, "was packing to go away. Is she going to be gone long?"

Oscar made no direct response to my question, but said, "Madam suggested that you might listen to reason."

"What is her idea of reason?" I asked.

"Madam is soft-hearted," he said disparagingly.

"It must," I said, "have wounded her tender heart when you committed two murders on her behalf."

"It is possible to be tender-hearted," he said, "but also to bow to necessity. Madam is fond of you, Mr. Applegate, so she insisted that you be given a chance to listen to reason."

"I repeat," I said, "what is Madam's idea of reason?"

"You know how much money was in the safe," he said.

"If," I answered, "I took that money I would count it. Naturally."

"Her orders to me," Oscar said, "were to offer what she called a reward for the return of lost property."

"A sort of sop to my conscience," I said. "How much is this reward?"

"One tenth," he said. "A hundred thousand dollars."

"Give up nine tenths and keep ten per cent!" I exclaimed derisively.

"I told her," Oscar said, "that you were no fool."

"Madam's house of cards," I said, "is ready to collapse. She made one fatal mistake."

Oscar shot his death's head forward as if the better to hear. "What mistake?" he asked.

"Jethro Willis," I said. "That slimy, cowardly, hand-rubbing scoundrel."

"I warned her," Oscar said. It was as if he admitted that I knew all the facts—was aware of the nature of Madam's fraud and chicanery.

"She should," I said, "have allayed his panic by a substantial payment. Now he's going to set the law in motion and you and Madam must skedaddle prematurely."

"Two hundred thousand," said Oscar.

I shook my head.

"Madam," he said, "is also very fond of Miss Lossie Fox."

I stood up suddenly, kicking my chair back so that it crashed to the floor, and stepped from behind my desk. There I stopped because Oscar had snatched a heavy-bladed knife from his overcoat pocket and was balancing it on his hand, ready for the throw.

"Oscar——" I said, and my voice was so oddly soft that I did not recognize it as my own. "Oscar, if you so much as lay a finger on Lossie, I'll kill you. You cannot go so fast or so far that I won't catch you and kill you with my hands."

I was surprised at the intensity of my rage; I was surprised that I could be so affected by a threat to Lossie.

"Will you give up the money?" he asked quietly.

"And bankrupt half a dozen banks! And bring poverty and want to hundreds of depositors, and calamity to all this part of the state!"

He swung his gaunt body toward the door, where he paused and spoke over his shoulder. "In one hour," he said gratingly, "you will have every dollar of that money at Madam's door. Or you will regret it to your dying day."

Then he was gone. I righted my chair. It would be nonsense to say that I was without apprehension, for Oscar was as deadly as a swamp rattler. As I stood leaning upon my desk, my duty became clear to me—my duty as an attorney and my obligation as a citizen. I would perform that duty quickly, and, having done so, I would then attend to matters more personal.

I put on my coat, hat and tippet and ran down the stairs and across the street to the bank over which Mr. Watts presided. I entered and strode back to his office, and, without asking permission, burst into the solemn privacy of his room. He rose from his chair, scowling.

"What does this intrusion mean, Orrin?" he demanded.

"It means," I said, "that you are a gullible, pompous ass." It was the truth, but even so, it was not proper for one of my age to speak so to a man of Mr. Watts' position and years.

"Get out of here, you impertinent puppy, before I have you thrown out neck and heels!"

"Before you do so," I said hotly, "look at the collateral Madam Janeway had deposited with you as security for her borrowing! Look at it as you should have done when you made the loan, and see if your credulity has not wrecked this bank!"

His mouth dropped open, his cheeks lost color and he gobbled in his throat, collapsing in his chair. I took it upon myself to step to the door and call the cashier of the institution.

"Mr. Watts," I said, "wants you to bring to him at once all Madam Janeway's papers, notes, collateral. At once."

In a matter of minutes the cashier put the papers

upon Banker Watts' desk. He goggled at them. "Open that sealed envelope," I ordered—and who was I, so young and untried a man, to venture such an audacity? But Banker Watts, hands shaking as with palsy, obeyed. He fumbled open the heavy envelope upon which was listed the securities to be found within, and the written signature of Dan'l Drew. The contents of the envelope spilled out upon his desk. He started at what lay under his eyes and uttered choking sounds and collapsed on the floor behind his desk. For the contents of the envelope were not stocks and bonds, but folded heavy blank paper.

I left him to be revived by someone else and to cope with his problem. I did not mention the million dollars I had taken from my safe and hidden aboard Lizzie Ann. I had but one thing on my confused mind then, and that was Lossie Fox. So, through the running gutters and slush, I hurried to Lossie's house and, like a privileged member of the family, opened the door without rapping and stood in the vestibule bellowing Lossie's name.

Mrs. Fox, wiping her hands on her apron, appeared from the kitchen and frowned at me. "Goodness gracious, Orrin! What's all the racket? Lossie isn't here. She went driving with Madam Janeway."

I turned without a mannerly word and rushed from the house. As I stood on the sidewalk I was possessed by a confused necessity to do something, but my brain would not inform me what to do. I could not think logically, nor reason, but stood helpless and bewildered. And then I heard hoofbeats and rounding the corner came

Madam Janeway's splendid carriage and team, with her coachman on his seat and Madam and Lossie under a rich fur robe, sitting red-cheeked and at their ease, chatting as if neither of them had a care in the world.

They turned into the driveway leading to the barn, but stopped under the porte-cochere. The ladies alighted and went into the house. It was all so normal and casual to the eye, but I knew it was not normal and casual. Lossie was a hostage for the return of a million dollars. Only by threatening her could Madam Janeway and Oscar compel me to surrender the loot which was the product of their scheming. And they had no time to lose.

I splashed across the street and up the steps. The door was not locked and I let myself in and called loudly, "Lossie, I'm here! It's all right, Lossie! I'm here!"

I strode into the back parlor where the ladies stood. They had not taken off their wraps. Lossie looked at me as if I had taken leave of my senses.

"Orrin Applegate!" she said angrily. "What's the meaning of this? What ails you?"

Madam Janeway smiled at me and then at Lossie. "Orrin thinks something is wrong," she said gently. And then, without change of expression or inflection, "Of course, Orrin is right. Something is quite, quite wrong. . . . We were expecting you, Orrin. Possibly not so soon."

Lossie was bewildered. "I don't understand," she said, looking from one to the other of us.

"Oscar," I said tersely, "found the safe empty."

"Oh!" said Lossie faintly.

"And the house of cards is tumbling down," I went on. "They've got to get back the money and run before they're caught in the ruins."

"Orrin," said Madam, and her voice was solicitous, "you really must be quick about it. We have no time to spare."

I almost said that they had less time than they thought. But I kept silent about my visit to Mr. Watts' bank and the discovery that Madam's collateral was blank paper.

"Come along, Lossie," I said. "Let's get out of here."

But Oscar's voice croaked behind me. "Nobody's going anywhere," he said, and advanced into the room. In his left hand—his big, splay-fingered left hand—he gripped a cluster of those throwing knives we had seen him practicing with in the barn. One of them was ready in his right hand.

"We've nothing to lose now, Orrin," Madam said. "We really must have that money, at any cost. It's terrible, Orrin, but it is necessary."

"As those two other murders were necessary!" I said. "The Duke, and was it—was it your brother?"

"It—it was heart-breaking," she said. "Heart-breaking."

"Shut up!" snarled Oscar.

She did not heed him. "But they made it necessary," she said. "They were blackmailers."

"The pot," said I, "calls the kettle black."

Oscar advanced a step into the room. "Your last chance!" he snarled. "Where is that money?"

Lossie had backed against the beautifully paneled wall. Her head was high and she was not afraid.

"Don't tell them," she said sharply.

Oscar's arm snapped back and flicked forward. The knife glinted through the air and buried its point in the oak an inch from Lossie's shoulder.

"Don't move!" I called in an agony of fear.

"The next one," Oscar said viciously, "will carve a piece of meat."

I faced Oscar. "If you so much as scratch her skin," I said evenly, "I'll kill you the way it hurts most."

"You," he retorted, "will be too dead to hurt a fly. For the last time, where is that money?"

"You'd better forget it," I said. "Banker Watts opened your envelope of stocks and bonds. You'd better run while you have a chance."

That shocked the man. His eyes widened, and I could see his shoulders sag and then stiffen. I was standing six feet to the left of Lossie, and near me was a solid wooden antique chair. In the instant of his shock I snatched it up and, leaping between him and Lossie, I presented it as a shield. Oscar hurled another knife, but it buried its point in the thick bottom of the chair. I crouched, pointing the chair legs toward him. Making myself as small as possible, I rushed upon him. I heard Madam scream, but there was no sound from Lossie.

A heavy chair with a broad bottom is not only a defensive but an offensive weapon. At close quarters it is frustrating to an antagonist—especially an antagonist with knives to throw. My unexpected rush threw Oscar back and pinned him against the wall. The four legs of the chair hampered and imprisoned him; the clumsy weapon could not be fended and skill was helpless against it.

Oscar had but one knife left and it was useless to him. I was very thankful for my size and strength, for I was able to wield my heavy weapon with ease. Suddenly I drew it back a scant six inches and jabbed with it viciously. Oscar grunted with pain as a leg punched him in the stomach, while another made contact with his shoulder.

Over my shoulder I called to Lossie, "Get out of here! Get out!" But I could not see if she obeyed. All I knew was that Oscar's arm must have been momentarily benumbed, for his remaining knife dropped to the carpet. But his recovery was quick, and his big hands clutched the chair and tried to wrestle it away from me. Gaunt though he was, there was tremendous strength in his arms and shoulders. He braced his back against the wall and, shifting his hold to two of the chair legs, twisted until the sturdy wood cracked and splintered and I found myself with only part of the seat and back—no longer an effective weapon. And even it, as we fought for its possession, disintegrated, leaving but a fragment in my hands and an equal fragment in his. And our bodies were in contact.

I thanked heaven for my friendship with the canawlers, whose delight it was to wrestle on the sward along the canal of evenings. They had taught me the tricks of catch-as-catch-can, and the dirtier twistings and gougings and kneeings intended to maim or even kill an adversary in serious and bloody battle.

But never had I encountered a strength equal to Oscar's strength save in one man only, and that was my friend, Zach Wheelright. We grappled, seeking the advantage of a punishing hold, stomping our feet so that the house shook with our trampling. We reeled about the room, toppling furniture, smashing glass and china, crashing into walls and rebounding, with neither having the advantage.

By common impulse we loosed each other and, crouching, circled with outstretched arms and clutching hands. Of a sudden, Oscar sent a kick at my kneecap, but I anticipated him by presenting my heel, and he cursed from the pain of it. I sidestepped to the right and stabbed at his eyes with stiffened fingers, but he danced away. It was not a fight with rules. There was no sportsmanship, no decency—only a grim intent to harm in any manner that hurt could be dealt. I was without compunction, for I knew that I was fighting for my life.

Once, as we whirled and sidestepped, I caught a glimpse of Lossie crouched against the wall, and of Madam, her fists pressed against her lips.

"I told you to get out!" I shouted.

"And let her stab you in the back!" Lossie cried.

How long we had been circling and straining, feinting and gripping, I did not know. But I did know that my heart pounded and my breath came in painful gulps. I was nearing the end of my string—and then I bethought me of a trick taught me by Zach. I lunged toward Oscar clumsily, pretended to trip and dropped to my knees. The maneuver requires split-second precision. By Oscar's re-action to my trick, I knew he was not familiar with it, for he aimed a kick at my face—and that was what I wanted. I was ready for it and avoided it, and as it whizzed past my ear I struck upward with all my strength. My hard fist went home on his groin and as he doubled in agony I surged up beneath him and lifted him from the floor. With every ounce of my remaining strength I hoisted him above my head, and then, as I had been taught, I spun upon my heels, once around, twice around, three times, and hurled Oscar, not to the floor, as I would have done had I been in the open, but headlong against the brickwork of the fireplace. The sound was a sound which I hope never to hear again—the cracking of a human skull. Oscar kicked once and lay still.

Madam screamed. She crouched in a corner, face hidden in her palms. Lossie did not crouch nor did she hide her face. She stood erect, shoulders back, and with such a look of elation as I never before beheld on a human face. She ran toward me, gripped my elbows and looked up into my face.

"You're the dandiest fighter alive!" she said, and then there was a pause and she said, "Why don't you kiss me, you great oaf?"

I never had kissed her. It never had occurred to me to do so; and the present moment seemed no time for it.

"Go along with you," I said. "I've no time for your monkeyshines now."

"When do you think you will have?" she asked meekly.

Madam Janeway spoke. She had dropped her hands from her face and was staring across the room at Oscar. Her cheeks were ashen and there was a wild look in her lovely eyes. "Is he dead?" she whispered.

"I hope so," said I, and was not surprised at my harshness. I had meant to kill him for what he had done to Lossie, and I felt no remorse.

"Oh, I hope so too. I hope so," Madam said wretchedly. "He was a horrid man. Horrid. I shall be free from him."

To that I did not reply, doubting its sincerity. Madam was a shifty, clever woman. Even in this tragic moment she might be preparing the way for her defense. She saw the possibility of shifting the blame to Oscar's shoulders and of assuming the role of an innocent, victimized woman. With her beauty, her dignity, her history of kindness and generosity, such a defense might be effective not only with the public but with a jury of her peers.

"He was your man," I said accusingly.

"He was my husband." There was hysteria in her voice. It was not a cultured voice now, but something common. "The shame of it!" she cried. "Chained to a thief and a murderer." She raised her eyes to mine and got to her feet, the picture of suffering innocence, of martyred womanhood. "Oh, Orrin, you will help me? You will advise me? You will stand by me in my hour of need?"

It was artificial, it was acting, but even though I recognized it for what it was, it affected me. I looked at Lossie and saw that she was crying. She was not crying from relief or as a result of fear. She was, I believe, crying for Madam Janeway, in bitter sorrow for what Madam Janeway might have been and for what she so tragically was. Lossie walked across the room and took the older woman in her arms to comfort her.

"I could have loved you so, and admired you so," she said to Madam. "There was so much that was fine and good. I'm crying because all that good must suffer along with the evil that was there too."

For a moment, Madam was natural, without acting or pretense.

"Little Lossie," she said, "I loved you."

"But," I said harshly, "you would have stood by and let Oscar murder her. You lured her here to torture her and make me tell where the money was hidden."

"But," Madam said softly, "it broke my heart."

That was acting; it was crafty insincerity. Whatever good Lossie saw in her or that I was able to perceive was in abeyance, and cunning and duplicity were in the ascendant.

"Orrin," she said in a piteous voice, "there is still time for me to escape. And you have all that money, Orrin. Help me to get away and I'll never tell. It will all be yours, Orrin—every penny will be yours!"

If my heart needed hardening that sufficed to turn it to steel.

"Madam," I said stonily, "I must ask you to come

with me."

"Where?" she asked, and her eyes pleaded with me.

"To the jail," I said.

"No!" cried Lossie. "Not you! You're not a police-man!"

But that decision was not to be mine. There was a clamor at the door, and it burst open and half a dozen men entered. In the lead was Banker Watts, whom I had seen last in a swoon on his office floor; there was our chief of police and men in uniform. They stopped sud-denly in the archway at the sight of Oscar and the pool of blood in which he lay.

"What's this? What's going on here?" our police chief demanded. And then Madam showed herself as she truly was, making one last, desperate effort. She pointed an accusing finger at me.

"That man," she said, "murdered my husband for the money. They plotted together to rob the banks. That man killed my husband so he could keep it all."

"That," said Lossie sturdily, "is a wicked lie."

Apparently none of them heeded Madam or Lossie. Banker Watts dominated them. He waved a yellow tele-graph blank and shouted, "What have you to say to this, you sharper, you thief? From Dan'l Drew! I wired him! This is his reply! 'The woman Janeway is an impostor. I never heard of her. I have had no relations with her. I will sue for slander any man who charges the con-trary.' " Watts was trembling with rage. "Impostor?" he roared. "Where's my money, woman? Where's my money?"

Jethro Willis, slinking in the rear, pasty-faced from fright, lifted a quavering voice, "Where's our money, woman? Where's our money?"

I could not keep scorn from my voice. "You deserve to lose your money," I said. "You were trusted by your depositors and you betrayed their trust. Gullible! Shamefully gullible! What precautions did you take? What investigations did you make? You let this woman beguile and bamboozle you. None of you—and you call yourselves bankers—so much as opened an envelope to see what it contained. But your money is safe. All but what Madam has spent in her career in Syracuse. Nearly a million dollars."

"Where is it? Where is it?" begged Watts and Willis.

"It's where Lossie Fox and I put it for safekeeping. It will be placed in the hands of proper authority. Let us proceed with order and decorum," I said, and stared down Banker Watts. "Not hysterically. Let Madam Janeway be taken into custody—and myself, if that be deemed necessary because of my killing of the man Oscar. Then call in the attorney general, for this matter ramifies through the state. There must be strict investigation and equitable division and restitution of this million dollars."

And so, because there was no other course to follow, it was done. Madam was confined, not in a cell, but in an apartment in the jail. Officials from Albany arrived and I, not yet placed under arrest, accompanied them to Lizzie Ann, where Zach Wheelright produced the satchelful of money.

In the end, hopeless and begging for clemency, Madam made full confession. She had been born in Connecticut and at the age of sixteen had run away from home. Even so young she exerted an amazing charm upon men. She married a doctor and disappeared with his bank account; she passed forged checks and served two terms in prison. She set up business as a fortuneteller and defrauded clients of considerable sums, but vanished before she could be brought to justice. She emerged again in Detroit, passing herself off as the daughter of a famous architect, and cashed some thousands of dollars of worthless checks. For a few years she lived quietly, until restlessness again drove her to seek excitement.

Another series of frauds made her take refuge with a patent-medicine show, where she sang songs to a banjo and allowed herself to stand before a plank while Oscar threw knives at her. She and Oscar were kindred spirits, and between them they planned the Dan'l Drew fraud, selecting Syracuse as remote from New York and a town of promising character.

Oscar demanded that she marry him, and from that date her life became a ghastly experience. He was a dangerous, deadly criminal. He had strangled the Duke because that man had tracked him down and was demanding a share of the loot. He had throttled Gideon Weeks, a brother of Madam's, for the same reason.

Madam was brought to trial and, though she produced a vigorous and clever defense, was convicted and sentenced to ten years in the state penitentiary.

I was given great credit for saving several banks from ruin—much more than I deserved. But, as Lossie said, it was silly to refuse gifts of the gods. Banker Watts, discredited in the city for his gullibility and carelessness, found it necessary to dispose of his bank holdings, which were bought by a coterie of citizens. And I, though younger than they would have had me, was given the position of the bank's attorney at law, a decently lucrative connection.

But, oddly enough, these tragic, melodramatic and sometimes humorous events did not bring to an end my connection with George Hull, cigar manufacturer of Binghamton, and the much-disputed Cardiff Giant.

* * 16 * *

IT would not be long now before navigation of
the canal reopened. Warm southern breezes softened the
imprisoning ice, and in the basin there was much activity
as the canawlers made ready their boats for the summer's
journeying. There was painting and calking and repair-
ing, and even gaiety as the men and women of the canal
emerged from their hibernation. Soon now there would
be rivalry for cargoes to be carried westward to Buffalo
or eastward to the Hudson River.

It was at this time that the newspapers of the country, probably because news had been in the doldrums,
interested themselves in the Cardiff Giant in a manner
they had not displayed hitherto. In the past their columns
had been filled with controversy, with arguments by
scientists and men of religion. Famous names had taken
their stands upon whether the giant was veritably a petrified man of ancient days, or a sculpture wrought by some
prehistoric artist. There had been those who proclaimed
it a fake, chief of whom was Andrew White, president of
Cornell. But personages of equal magnitude made elaborate statements averring that it was a marvelous and

ancient work of art. All but religious fanatics seemed to have abandoned the belief that it had once been a man walking the earth and breathing the air. The public still flocked to pay their money to stare at it. And people still passed their dollars through the window to peer at Barnum's imitation of the original giant.

But now the controversy took a different turn. Able newspapermen forsook the religious or scientific aspects of the man of stone to do a real job of detection—to discover how the giant came to be interred in Stubby Newell's farm; where it came from and by what means it arrived. And to identify, if possible, the stone carver who had wrought it.

In rapid succession new facts came to light. Circumstantial and eyewitness evidence was adduced until it seemed as if the veritable story of the hoax would soon be exposed in its entirety.

One morning George Hull, the agnostic cigar manufacturer, came to my office and occupied the client's chair.

"Mr. Applegate," he said, "I'm kind of, sort of, after a fashion, worried about haow I stand."

"With respect to what?" I asked.

"The giant," he said. "Too much is bein' unearthed. It won't be long naow before the papers publish all about it. What I come to consult you about, Mr. Applegate, is haow I stand legal."

"You are worried," I said, "as to whether a criminal prosecution can be brought against you for fraud or for obtaining money under false pretenses."

"That's the ticket," he said. He did not seem to be acutely worried.

"Did you ever state orally or in print that the effigy was once a living man? That it was a petrified giant that once had been flesh and blood?"

"Never," he said firmly.

"Did you ever state that it was an ancient statue, a Phoenician sculpture or otherwise of great age?"

"Not once," he answered, and grinned. "I just left fools to draw their own conclusions. I didn't have to make statements. All I had to do was stand by and let them make fools of themselves. It kind of give me satisfaction to watch 'em squabble." His expression was saturnine. "There's no nonsense so silly but what folks will credit it as truth. Ye don't have to lie to them, Mr. Applegate. Just give 'em a chance and they'll swaller anything whole. They jest naturally crave to be gulled. Like in this Madam Janeway business."

"Would you care to tell me the whole truth about it?" I asked.

"I've had my fun and made me a snag of money. I'm ready to tell it to the world. And have the laugh on 'em. Parsons and scientists! I showed 'em up for what they be."

"Very well," I said. "Start at the beginning."

He settled himself in his chair and squinted at me maliciously. "Wa-al," he said, "it all come about kind of by chance. I was visitin' my sister out in Ioway, and there was one of them shoutin' evangelists apreachin'. Not makin' sense. He bellered out that there was giants in them days, and I stood up and demanded to know how big them giants was. He was took back, but all the same he answered up and says that they was ten feet high."

Hull grinned impishly and took a chew of tobacco. He was enjoying himself in a sardonic way.

"I got to mulling it over and it come to me I could have my fun and mebby make some money. So I swapped a keg of beer to a feller for a great big block of gypsum. I was ready to invest some money in making folks look small, even if there was no profit in it. So I got the hunk of gypsum lugged to Chicago, where I got a graveyard sculptor on North Clark Street. He whittled out the giant to my specifications, and made it look real by peckin' tiny holes all over it, like the pores in a man's skin. And on its back I had him cut channels like it was worn by runnin' water."

"Thorough," I observed.

"The tough job was luggin' it to Stubby's farm," he said. "It busted down wagons 'n' it caved in bridges. But I got it there and buried it 'n' left it to ripen for a year. Then Stubby dug it up. Then the fun started."

"Now you're a little worried lest your fun result in criminal prosecution?"

"Not too much, but I be a mite uneasy."

"Mr. Hull," I said, "I can inform you that you are guilty of nothing criminal. You made no guarantees. You just stood by and reaped your harvest. You only let the public draw their own conclusions."

"Which," he said, "they done. Confirming my view

that human beings is just eager to get gouged, and willing to fight and bleed for any doggone fool idee, whether it's religion or politics or the layin' on of hands to cure disease. Yup. The's jest one quality all created human beings share. And that, Mr. Applegate, is gullibility."

"So," I was forced to agree, "it would seem. And what are your plans now, Mr. Hull?"

"I figger, since I hain't liable to no pains or penalties, to tell the whole story to the papers. And git my last big laugh out of it."

And that is what George Hull proceeded to do. And, weirdly enough, the result of it was to increase the size of the crowds who thronged to see the giant. And what was strangest of all, to confirm the belief of religious fanatics that the stone man was indeed created by God and was a miracle from heaven.

Every day the opening of the canal drew nearer, and at last word came through from east and west that the big ditch was free of ice. Lossie and I decided to go down to the basin to say good-by to Lizzie Ann and to Zach and his woman.

We were going to a musicale, which was a social occasion that required dressing in our best. Our fathers and mothers were to go in our carriage, so Lossie and I were permitted the use of the Fox buggy and we left after an early supper, so that we could visit the Wheelrights before the evening's entertainment began.

Lossie certainly was not my little playmate that night. She wore a gown that she had bought while on her travels, and her hair was piled elaborately on her head, with little curls escaping as though by accident, but actually with shrewd calculation. She wore dainty little slippers and a gold chain about her neck with a locket hanging from it. As she came into the dining room she was radiant and dignified, like a princess out of a fairy tale. This she knew, and looked at me smugly.

I thought to take her down a peg, so I said, "You wouldn't jump off your porch railing into a pile of leaves in that getup."

She twitched her nose at me and arranged her skirts with their hoops, and a fan dangled from a ribbon at her wrist. Her expression was prim, and did not change, even though she brought the heel of her slipper down upon my instep so that I winced.

She smiled in a sardonic way and said, "How dignified and splendid you look tonight, Orrin! Almost too grown up. I do hope you don't split your coat."

I was unhappily aware that since that coat had been bought my shoulders had widened, and the sleeves were a trifle too short, and it angered me that she should treat me as if I were some hobbledehoy of half her age.

"Anyhow, I'm not a scrawny little brat that wouldn't make a mouthful for a crow," I said snappishly.

"Scrawny?" she said and elevated her brows in a superior manner. "I'd have you know that I'm not scrawny, but slender, and that my figure has been commented upon favorably by gentlemen of experience and perception."

I had not seen much of Lossie since that day in Madam Janeway's parlor when I had fought with Oscar and when Lossie, being upset by the fighting, had asked me to kiss her. I don't know that she had avoided me, but she did seem to be very busy and to have little time for me. And when she did see me she was always aloof and hoity-toity, as if we were comparative strangers instead of play-fellows from babyhood.

Tonight she was no different. We got up from the table and I handed her into the buggy, which awaited us in the driveway. I tucked the lap robe about her, and she said, "Scrawny," under her breath.

"Well," I told her, "you can't help it. Legs like a couple of broomsticks! Chasing after me like a grasshopper!"

"That," she said furiously, "was years ago! Girls grow up and—and their legs change!"

"Yours," I said, "would have to change a lot."

"Not only," she said, "are you a great, clumsy ox, Orrin Applegate, but you've cataracts in both eyes. And no gumption. It doesn't make any difference how modest a girl is, any man with the slightest bit of git-up-and-git to him will have stolen peeks at her legs."

"I'm not interested," I told her.

After that there was a chill in the air until I had driven the buggy as near to the Lizzie Ann as was possible, and I cramped the wheels and walked around to help her alight. She jumped down all by herself and almost slipped and fell on her nose, and I said "Smarty," and she stuck out her tongue at me.

We went aboard the Lizzie Ann and I let out a holler to tell Zach Wheelright and his woman that we were there. Zach opened the door, and welcoming light poured out from the cabin and an agreeable odor of coffee and baking.

"Come in and welcome!" he bellowed, and reaching up his great hands he swung Lossie down the steps and into the cabin. "We was afraid we'd have to go 'thout seeing you agin."

Zach's woman was holding her close and calling her Lizzie Ann and tears were running down her thin and leathery cheeks. Lossie took off her wraps and stood there in her finery.

Zach goggled at her with eyes as big as saucers, and said, "Maw, fur goodness' sake, look! Our leetle gal's growed up!"

"I took note fur some time," Maw said dryly, "that she's been aworkin' up to it. The's been visible signs that she's left childhood behind and has got to be a woman. My leetle Lizzie Ann, a woman growed and ready fur marryin' 'n' babies and all." She dabbled at her beady bright eyes and patted Lossie. "Soon she'll be gittin' her a man, Zach, and we'll be losin' our leetle gal."

"You'll never lose me, Maw," Lossie said gently.

And then Maw Wheelright turned her bright eyes upon me and said sourly, "Heaven knows you've growed up, Orrin Applegate. But big as you be, ye hain't growed up as much as her." She frowned at me. "I suppose ye hain't had sense to make up your mind yit or to see what's what."

"Make up my mind about what, Maw Wheelright?" I asked.

"Some," Maw said to Lossie, "is dumber'n what others be. This one, he takes the prize."

"He is stupid," Lossie said, and nodded for emphasis.

"Ye hain't contrived to make him come to scratch?" Maw asked.

Lossie spoke like a little girl, and you could almost see her wriggle and play with the strings of her pinafore. "I'd rather," she said in a low voice, "that he came to scratch all by himself."

Zach roared with Homeric laughter. "Proba'ly," he said, "the boy's been thataway for a long time, but hain't woke up to it. Some folks need nudgin'."

"He's so thick-skinned," Lossie said, "that he doesn't notice nudges."

"Set daown," Maw commanded me. I did so, and she stood in front of me bristling like an angry bantam hen. "Look ye here, Orrin Applegate. Ye been arunnin' around with our Lizzie Ann since ye both was babies."

"Yes'm," I said. "We're next-door neighbors."

"The time's full ripe," she went on inexorably, "when her folks is bounden to ax ye what is your intentions?"

"My intentions!" I exclaimed.

"Let's start easy and elementary," Maw said. "Do ye deem Lizzie Ann to be a handsome gal?"

"Why, yes, Maw. Lossie's all right."

"Look at her," Maw commanded. "Look at her where she stands there all decked out in silks 'n' satins, like a princess."

I did so. There was no doubt that Lossie was as

lovely as a girl could be. I did not look into her eyes, but a very pleasant sort of excitement took possession of me.

"Think back," Maw said peremptorily. "Call to mind the day when ye feared harm had come to her. Call to mind how ye felt that day."

"I call it to mind very clearly," I said.

"To be sure," Maw went on. "And that day ye fought 'n' killed a dangerous bad man. With her alookin' on. Why did ye do so, Orrin?"

"Because I hated him," I said hotly.

"So-oo-oo!" Maw exclaimed. "And why did ye hate him, boy?"

"Because I——" I said and stopped. "Because," I went on in a second, "he dared to threaten her and frighten her. And because I'd tear apart any man that dared so much as lay a finger on her to harm her." I stopped again and looked at Maw Wheelright, and then across at Lossie, and I took a stride toward my girl, and I said in a big voice, "You don't need to ask me why I'd do that. You don't need to prompt me any more. The reason for it," I said, and my voice grew smaller, "is that she's the most precious thing in the world to me, and I wouldn't want to stay alive if she left me in the world alone."

Then I ventured to look at Lossie, and her eyes were wet, but behind the tears they were very lovely and yearning; and her sweet lips were parted, and there was an expression there that was not a smile, but was more splendid than a smile. And slowly she lifted her hands toward me until her arms were outstretched.

I heard Zach Wheelright say to his woman, "Woman, I calc'late we best go bide on deck."

So those two fine friends turned their backs on us and left us alone in their warm, cozy cabin.

I stood there a little time, and then I said to her, "Playmate, what a great, blind oaf I've been!"

And she nodded her head in agreement and came a step nearer. "But," she said softly, "the dandiest great oaf that ever was."